RETRIBUTION
RIDGE

A dark, gripping and intense suspense thriller

ANNA WILLETT

Paperback edition published by

The Book Folks

London, 2017

© Anna Willett

This book is a work of fiction. Names, characters, businesses, organizations, places and events are either the product of the author's imagination or are used fictitiously. Any resemblance to actual persons, living or dead, events or locales is entirely coincidental. The spelling is British English.

All rights reserved. No part of this publication may be reproduced, stored in retrieval system, copied in any form or by any means, electronic, mechanical, photocopying, recording or otherwise transmitted without written permission from the publisher.

ISBN 978-1-9735-7291-6

www.thebookfolks.com

For my husband Craig and my daughters Monica and Grace. Your unfailing love and support keeps me going.

Chapter One

"You didn't have to agree." Harper pulled her hair back and fastened it with a black band. "You could have just said no."

A good point. One her friend had made at least eight times since leaving Perth. Millicent could have told her sister she had work commitments – not completely untrue. Hell, she could have just flatly refused. Two days hiking the Cape to Cape trail wasn't her idea of a holiday. But Judith's offer of some sisterly bonding time was the first real attempt either of them had made at a reconciliation since Mum's funeral. How could she say no?

"I know. And believe me, I'd rather reconnect over cocktails in Bali, but …" Milly paused, and rubbed the back of her neck. "You know how prickly Judith can be. If I'd said anything but yes, I wouldn't have heard from her for another ten years." She sighed. "I'm glad you agreed to come along as a buffer."

"Okay, well, stop complaining and make the best of it."

Milly glanced over and fixed her friend with a grimace. She was right. She'd accepted Judith's offer so now it was time to suck it up and mend some fences. Even if it meant sleeping on the ground and peeing in the bushes. But was roughing it really the problem? Seeing Judith again, being reminded of the things Milly had worked so hard to leave in the past – just thinking about it made her stomach twist in an unpleasant knot.

"And watch the road," Harper added pointing at the windscreen.

Ahead, packed on either side by towering gums and scraggy natives, it narrowed to two lanes curving left. Milly eased her foot off the accelerator and glanced down at the navigation screen. The turn off for the Breaker's Ledge carpark showed as less than a kilometre ahead.

"Last night I dreamed of the Reach." She hadn't meant to say anything but the words spilled out.

"Don't, Milly."

"Don't what?" The question came out as a moan.

"Don't get bogged down in all that." Harper waved her arm in an expansive gesture, her tone sharp with impatience. "Especially not now. You and Judith need to work out how you can build a relationship *now*." She jabbed her index finger in a downward motion. "Bringing up the tragedy that tore you apart is counterproductive, unless there's anything about that night that needs rehashing?"

Milly felt uneasy. What was Harper getting at? *Stop it*, she told herself. *She's not getting at anything. No need to get paranoid.* "No. No… It was just a dream." Milly pressed her lips together. She shouldn't have mentioned it. Dredging up the past would only taint any chance she had of moving forward with her sister.

They rounded the bend and the dense bush fell away as the road began its gradual ascent. With the windows cracked, the smell of salt and dried seaweed filled the car.

"I'd say we're getting close."

"Smells like it," Harper seemed excited by the prospect of a few days in the great outdoors.

"It's not like you to be happy about giving up your creature comforts," Milly teased.

"You've been away for a long time, Milly." Harper shrugged. "Things change."

True, Milly had left Perth ten years ago and moved to Sydney. But she'd kept in touch. Not constantly, but at least once a month. *I probably could try harder.*

"Harper, I…"

"There it is." Harper leaned forward and tapped the dashboard. "We're here."

Fine whitish-grey sand mounds lined the edges of the road, as if forcing back the human intrusion. A low fence of pine logs zig-zagged into the parking lot. Milly pulled in, taking care to stop between the white lines in the almost empty lot.

Before Milly had time to turn the engine off, Harper bounced out of the car and headed towards the silver four-wheel drive parked three spaces away. She watched her friend bound over to Judith and pull her into a quick hug. Judith's arms came up, but didn't quite make it around Harper's back. She hesitated just long enough for Harper to let her loose and turn her attention to the man standing at the rear of the vehicle.

Milly could hear Harper say something, but her attention was fixed on Judith. It had been three months since their mother's funeral. They'd barely spoken at the chapel. Sitting on the same bench separated by their cousin and his wife, Milly snatched glimpses of her sister as Mum's coffin began its descent to the crematorium. Only once did Judith look away and meet Milly's gaze. For a moment, her sister's eyes held a look of anguish and desperation. Milly wanted to put her arms around her and make everything better. Then Judith straightened her back and clenched her jaw. She turned away and the moment vanished.

Now Judith regarded her with the same clenched jaw and accusing glare. Milly lifted her hand in a wave that felt stiff and awkward. The wind ruffled Judith's brown hair. She raised her hand in what might have been a greeting, but turned into an attempt to push her fringe out of her eyes.

"This is going to be a long two days." Milly sighed and climbed out of the car.

"I'm Lucas. Lucas Werd. A friend of Judith's. She's asked me to lead the hike."

"I'm Milly. I see you've met Harper." Milly grasped the man's hand, grateful that he'd stepped forward and bridged the uncomfortable silence between her and Judith.

"I was just telling Lucas that you and Judith haven't really spoken in years, not since you were both teenagers. So," Harper drew out the word. "This might be the most tortuous hiking group he's ever led."

Harper's words hung in the air. Milly felt the knot in her stomach twist into full-blown anxiety. *Why did I agree to this*, she asked herself, and not for the first time. Guilt? Loneliness? She wanted to look at her sister and see how the moment was affecting her, but she couldn't bear to meet Judith's gaze. She found her eyes darting everywhere but at the one person she'd driven three hours to see.

"What's all the rope for?" Her focus landed on the pile of equipment heaped on the bitumen near the rear of the car.

"We're going to do a bit of abseiling." It was the first time Judith had spoken since Milly and Harper arrived.

Milly forced herself to meet her sister's gaze. Judith's blue eyes were shiny, as if filled with unshed tears. There were tiny lines creasing her forehead and the softness Milly remembered seemed absent from her face. Although it had been only three months since the funeral, it had been almost ten years since she'd really looked at her sister. The changes were unsettling.

"Judith, I… Hi."

"Hi." Something flickered across Judith's face. It could have been the beginnings of a smile, but the look vanished and Judith turned to Lucas. "When everything's ready we should get going. It's almost ten." She moved to the back of the vehicle, pulled a large red pack out and dropped it on the ground. "If you need to use the loo, the toilet block's over there." She jerked her head towards a squat brick building in the left hand corner of the sandy carpark.

"Okay. After that heart-warming reunion, I need to pee." Harper headed for the toilet block.

Milly followed her friend. Harper jogged across the bitumen, her long blonde ponytail bouncing up and down on her shoulders. Milly didn't bother to try to keep pace, she walked slowly, relishing a few moments away from the painful exchange with her baby sister. Agreeing to this trip had been a mistake from the beginning. *What was I thinking?* It seemed like a great idea via email, with thousands of kilometres separating them. In person, nothing had changed. They were both still angry and hurt; this trip might only make it worse.

Milly stepped into the toilet block. The floor was a faded grey concrete slab and the walls exposed brick. A building typical of bland, functional, Australian beach-side conveniences, she could have been standing in any such block on any beach in the country.

"Harper?" Milly crossed the overly spacious room and stood in front of the closed stall door. "I wish you'd just tone it down a bit. It's difficult enough without you constantly pointing out the awkwardness of the situation."

"I'm just trying to lighten the mood," Harper's voice echoed from behind the door. "You two need to thaw out and start talking or this is never going to work."

"That's just it." Milly looked down at her shoes and let her shoulders drop. "It's not working. There's too much pain and … I don't know. I think it's better if I call it quits now and leave."

The door swung inward and Harper darted forward with such speed, Milly wondered if her friend had been standing on the other side. A weird thought, one that she instantly dismissed.

"What do you mean leave? We drove three hours and have been here approximately ten minutes." Harper took a step closer. "Now you want to just turn around and drive back to Perth?"

Milly felt taken aback by Harper's reaction. But then she'd asked her friend to come and act as a shock absorber while the sisters tried to patch things up. She really couldn't blame her for being pissed off at being jerked around.

"Look, I know I asked you to come as a favour and you've put things on hold to be here. But you saw what it was like out there." Milly gestured over her shoulder. "Maybe some things can't be fixed."

Harper grabbed Milly's arm and glared up at her. "No. We're doing this." In the dimness, her blue eyes looked almost black. "This might be your last chance to get your sister back in your life, and I'm not letting you give up after ten minutes."

Harper's fingers dug into Milly's arm with surprising strength. *Maybe she's right. Did I really expect Judith to rush into my arms and act like that night never happened?* Her knee-jerk reaction was to run away, just like she'd done last time.

"It's only two nights," Harper's voice softened. She let go of Milly's arm. "Didn't Judith say it was what your mum wanted, for you two to try again?"

At the mention of her mother, Milly weakened. In Judith's email she'd said their mother made her promise to try again. She wanted her girls to be close again. She could at least try, if only for her mother's sake.

"Yes. You're right." Milly nodded. "Ignore me, I'm just having a moment." She managed a weak smile and touched her friend's hand. "Thank you for being the voice of reason."

"Don't mention it." Harper returned the smile and headed for the exit. "Don't be too long in here, we need to get going," she called over her shoulder.

In the distance, the moan of the ocean and the screeching of seagulls merged in a frantic chorus.

Chapter Two

He watched the small, white hatchback pull into the carpark. He didn't bother to slide down in his seat, people seldom took in anything outside of their immediate focus. Besides, he'd parked at the far end and the windows were tinted. He felt relaxed, self-assured in his anonymity. He watched the blonde spring out of the car, tapping his fingers on the bottom of the steering wheel in an excited tempo. Small, slim, nice legs. She held his interest for no more than a few seconds. It was the tall dark one he'd been waiting to see.

She climbed out of the car, long-limbed and confident. It had been a long time, but she hadn't really changed. A little older, but still the same arrogant rich girl used to getting her own way. He gripped the steering wheel and looked down at his lap. His breathing slowed. He calmed himself by picturing the smug look slide into terror when she finally understood what was happening to her. A smile crept over his face; it held no warmth or merriment.

Boots crunching on the tightly packed pea stones around the toilet block snapped him out of his reverie. The blonde jogged past the grimy windscreen. She tossed her head, almost looking his way. He cocked his chin to the side, the smile still lifting his coarse features. Her shorts hugged her toned ass, cupping the firm, round mounds. Smooth, tanned legs revealed up to mid-thigh. She'd be an added bonus; he'd have some fun with Blondie. Maybe draw it out a bit. It wasn't part of his plan, but why not? He had plenty of time.

The dark-haired one strode past and his smile soured. She'd be the main event. Something to be savoured; his moments with her stored up for future examination. He watched Millicent turn the corner and disappear into the toilet block. He'd have liked to slip out of the car to skirt the building, maybe listen to the two women talking. He imagined their private schoolgirl voices, high and superior. *What will they sound like when they're screaming?* He stayed put behind the wheel and turned his attention to the sister.

The years *had* changed Judith; hardened her in a way he couldn't quite put his finger on. She had the air of an athlete, someone who'd spent years training and wanted to show the world what they could do. She pushed her body away from the car, folded her arms and tilted her head up as if searching the sky for divine answers. Her stance looked impatient. *Can't wait for it all to get going.* He almost laughed. *Me too, Judith. I'm raring to go*.

When the group gathered back together, he watched them pick up their stuff and set off. Leaning sideways, he reached under the passenger seat, his fingers hooking around the handle of the knife. Drawing it out, he took a moment to examine it. The blade picked up a glint of sunlight that reflected back in his face. He imagined Blondie's face when he showed her the knife, and chuckled. *She'll be a scared rabbit.*

He forced his thoughts back to the present and carefully slid the blade into the sheaf fastened to the small of his back. He checked the time on his watch: just past ten. An hour's head start should be enough. He decided to recline the seat and take a nap. The knife pressed into his back, the feeling brought him comfort. He closed his eyes and imagined himself with the blonde. His business was with the sisters, but she was something.

"Let the good times roll," he whispered before drifting off to sleep.

Chapter Three

Twenty minutes into their two-day hike, Milly began to relax. The sea breeze lifted her hair and played across the back of her neck. Overhead, the almost cloudless sky stretched out in an endless expanse of blue. She filled her lungs with tangy sea air and tilted her face to the sun. She'd worried that being this close to the sea with Judith would rattle her, but so far the dark memories kept their distance.

"Not bad out here, is it?" Harper asked from behind her.

They walked single file with Lucas in the lead, followed by Judith, then Milly, and Harper in the rear.

"No. Not bad at all." Milly slowed her progress on the red sandy path that led them along the top of the long white beach. The contrasting colours made her feel as if she were on another planet. "Walking through soft sand for two days will do wonders for my thighs."

"We'll be looping back inland in another hour or so," Lucas called from his place at the head of the group. "The terrain will be less sandy, but still challenging."

"Oh. I thought the Cape to Cape ran mostly along the beach?" Milly stopped walking and readjusted the straps of her backpack. "I didn't realise we'd be in the bush."

Judith stopped and turned to face her sister. She wore a floppy blue hat and sunglasses making it difficult to read her expression. "Not afraid of spending the night in the bush, are you?"

"Why should I be?" Milly snapped back before she could stop herself and cringed. The question sounded much harsher than she intended.

If Judith was bothered by her tone, she didn't show it. "No reason." She shrugged and continued walking.

Milly watched her sister's back. Judith looked slim. Slimmer than she'd been as a teenager. She wore loose, khaki shorts and a long-sleeved denim shirt. Her legs were tanned and muscular. Milly wondered if the muscles were from hours at the gym or days spent hiking. She had a flash of memory – Judith in yellow bathers, ten years old and chubby. They were at the beach, probably Cottesloe. Judith held her hand and together they jumped over waves laughing with excitement and waiting for the surf to knock them off their feet.

The image faded. Milly realised she knew nothing about her sister as an adult. All she had were memories, and even those seemed like dreams. Suddenly the cries of the seagulls rang mournful and depressing. Milly bit her bottom lip and blinked away tears. *Maybe we can build some new memories*, she thought and watched her sister stride confidently over a patch of reddish sand. The colour reminded Milly of dried blood. She looked back at the powdery white beach in the distance and felt a moment's trepidation. *I'm being ridiculous*, she told herself. *The colour's nothing more than some kind of mineralisation due to the surrounding granite. Australia's covered in red sand, I can't let every little thing get under my skin.* She took a deep breath and tried to focus on matching her stride with Judith's.

The path got steeper and Milly found herself sweating in spite of the crisp sea breeze. "Lucas, can we stop for a minute and take a break?"

Judith dropped her pack on the path. It was an impatient movement. She flopped down in the sand and swiped her hat off.

"Okay," Lucas stopped and pulled a sheaf of papers out of one of the many pockets on his long pants. "We're nearly at the edge of the cliffs." He shuffled the papers and slipped them back in his pocket.

Lucas's deep, masculine voice competing with the sough of the ocean triggered a long suppressed memory – jagged rocks gleaming like alien pieces of obsidian in the moonlight. White skin, stark and helpless. Milly shuddered and forced her mind back to the present.

She slipped her shoulders out of her pack and sat a metre or so away from her sister. Harper stepped around them and stood beside Lucas. She seemed quite taken with him. *Just like Harper*, Milly smiled in amusement, *zeroing in on the nearest available man.*

"We need to talk." Judith pulled a bottle of water from the side of her pack and unscrewed the cap.

Milly's tongue felt sandy and dry. She reached for her water bottle hoping Judith meant talk about the future, not the past.

"Probate will be finalised this week. I think we should keep Mum's house and rent it out."

It wasn't what Milly had been expecting. Not what she'd hoped for. Was this why Judith wanted the get together? To talk about finalising their mother's substantial estate? Surely not, they could have done that just as well by email. Still, it surprised her that financial matters were the first thing Judith brought up. A flicker of resentment sparked in her gut. Maybe she thought getting her out here and badgering her would be a better approach.

"Is that why we're here?" she snapped. "You want to sort out the money?"

Judith flinched and Milly immediately felt guilty for her outburst. "No. That's not why we're here. I…" Judith's voice trailed off. "Sorry. Not the best way to start off." Judith put her hat on and shoved her drink bottle back in her pack. "It's just hard to know *where* to start."

The emotion in her sister's voice struck a chord. Milly wanted this to work. She wanted it more than she'd realised. Seeing Judith again brought up bad memories, but good ones too. Maybe it could never be like it was before that night, but just to know they weren't enemies would be something.

"No, *I'm* sorry. I shouldn't have snapped at you." Milly thought of touching her sister's arm but hesitated. "I know we have to start somewhere, how about something a bit lighter?"

"Like what?" Judith asked with a small raise of her lips.

Milly pushed her straw hat back and scratched her sweat-dampened fringe. "Tell me about work. How's it going?" Milly knew Judith worked for a big law firm but not much else.

"It's okay." She shrugged. "Not very interesting. I'm mostly in the Human Resource Department. You?"

"Same. Nothing terribly exciting." Milly felt a small flutter in her stomach. She wished she hadn't brought up work. Worried that she'd let too much slip, she tried to be evasive. "I do enjoy my work, it certainly keeps me busy…"

"Oh come on. We all know you're a big successful magazine editor." Judith chuckled, but her tone carried an edge of bitterness. "You don't have to play it down for us mere mortals." She waved her hand towards Lucas and Harper who had stopped talking and were now listening to the sister's conversation.

"I'm not playing it down." Milly knew she sounded defensive and tried to smile. "I'm an assistant editor. Not *the* editor."

"I'm sure it won't take you long to get to the top," Judith said and stood.

"Okay girls." Harper trilled. "Play time's over. Let's keep going."

Milly scrambled to her feet and followed the group. Only now Harper was at the front with Lucas and she was left to bring up the rear. For a moment they'd seemed to be actually talking, then everything changed and Judith shut down again. *What did I say? Is it going to be like this the whole time?* She felt the spark of resentment reignite. *I'm not the one who got someone killed. Why should I always feel like the bad guy?*

* * *

Judith watched Lucas stomp along the path as it edged its way above the jagged cliffs. Far below, the sound of the surf exploded against the rocks. Being this close to the water with Millicent unnerved her. The skin on her arms felt tender with pickles that rubbed against the fabric of her shirt. Her thoughts constantly shifted between the past and present, keeping her off balance and jumpy. *Once we veer away from the coast, I'll feel better*, she told herself.

From the moment Milly got out of her car, Judith felt her disquiet increase. It was only the beginning of the journey, they had a long way to go. She wondered if she could keep her anger in check until she reached her goal. She had to keep calm and find a way to talk to her sister without giving anything away. She wondered how Harper was feeling and resisted the urge to stop and watch her move along the trail.

"We're heading inland now, so the going might get rough," Lucas called over his shoulder and stepped off the path.

Barely listening, Judith followed Lucas off the trail toward the barren landscape that separated the coast from the forest.

Underfoot, the sand turned to granite and then greyish dust. Judith could hear her sister behind her, walking boots thumping and scraping along the track. *I wonder how long she'll last before she wants another rest?* She wanted things to speed up. For this to have any chance of working, they had to reach the cliff.

Chapter Four

Milly swallowed the last of her Vegemite sandwich with a sip of water. The sky hung like a milky blue curtain scattered with wispy strands of cloud. With some distance between them and the coast, the wind calmed to a cool breeze.

"How long have you and Judith known each other?" Milly asked, crumpling up the wax paper wrapping from her sandwich and stowing it in a zip lock bag.

Lucas took a bite of a bruised-looking green apple and chewed slowly. Milly began to think he wasn't going to answer. "Not long," he finally said.

Milly noticed dark lines curling out across his chest. It looked like a word tattooed beneath his shirt but she couldn't make out the letters. *Probably one of those hipster inspirational tattoos like Carpe Diem or Breathe,* she thought and suppressed the urge to smile.

"So what do you do when you're not leading hiking groups?" She tried to draw him out in the hope of finding out what sort of person her little sister hung out with.

"I'm a personal trainer," his voice rasped deep, almost husky and his eyes looked so dark, they seemed bottomless.

Milly wondered if there might be more between him and her sister than friendship. But if that were the case, why would he spend so much time chatting to Harper? And why was he being so monosyllabic? What had Judith told him? She watched him suck on the apple core and then toss it in his mouth and chew it up. She wrinkled her nose and pushed up off the rough slab of granite.

Judith stood away from the group, beneath a scattering of gum trees. Her hat tucked in her back pocket, one hand on her hip while she ate one of Lucas's green apples. Milly decided it might be a chance to have a word in private with her sister. As she walked away, she heard Lucas explaining the importance of secure knots to Harper. *God, he really is a bit of an ass.*

"I thought you hated green apples." It was the first thing that popped into Milly's mind, she hoped it didn't sound critical.

"Yeah." Judith screwed up her nose in a familiar expression. "I don't know why I'm forcing it down." She tossed the apple into the trees where a magpie immediately pounced on it and hopped away with the half-eaten piece of fruit in its pointy beak. "I notice you still love your Vegemite." She seemed to be about to say something else but stopped.

"Some things never change." Milly watched the bird dance amongst the trees. "I'm sorry about earlier. You know, if I said something to upset you." She spoke without looking at her sister. "I really want this to work out. I want us to be friends." The words were out. She steeled herself for a rebuff or glib comment.

"I do too and I'm sorry for being so … prickly." The tremor in Judith's voice surprised her, as did her willingness to admit she was also at fault. "I'm glad you have a great career, it's just…" Judith sighed. "I suppose I feel a bit…"

"Alright, let's get moving," Lucas's voice made Milly jump. *How had he approached them so silently?*

Milly thought about protesting, but Judith was already walking back to her pack, the moment lost.

* * *

The afternoon drew on, the light dimmed, and the sun settled behind gathering clouds. Milly checked her watch: 3:15 p.m. They'd been heading inland for three hours. The landscape had transformed from squat, succulent scrub to increasingly barren granite. Her pack, manageable at first, now felt as if a couple of bricks had been added. Her shoulders protested at the weight and the straps bit into the soft skin around her collar bone. She considered asking for another break, but no one else seemed to be struggling so she gritted her teeth and pushed on.

"I need a toilet break." Judith didn't wait for permission. She dropped her pack and took off into the bush.

"Alright," Lucas said mostly to Harper. "We may as well stop for a few minutes."

His attitude was starting to wear on Milly. They'd been walking for hours and he'd barely acknowledged her. Come to think of it, he'd hardly spoken to Judith either. Milly slipped off her pack and let lose a moan of relief. She rolled her shoulders and stretched her neck to the side.

"How you doing, Mil?" Harper asked. Apart from a light sheen of perspiration on her upper lip, she looked unfazed by the hike.

Milly kneaded her shoulder. "I'm beginning to think I'm out of my depth," she whispered. "I'm not a marathon runner like you."

"I'll tell Lucas to slow down a bit." Harper kneaded Milly's other shoulder. "This is meant to be fun, not a death march."

Milly started to speak, but Harper's choice of words took her breath away. *A death march.* The words sent a chill up her arms. She rolled the sleeves of her shirt down and fastened them at her wrists. The breeze that had been crisp and refreshing at first, now felt harsh and stinging. She looked around for her sister, but she'd disappeared into the ragged-looking bush.

Milly listened to Harper and Lucas discussing the pace of their hike. "I don't think we should push it," Harper stood a few metres away with her back to Milly. "Let's just keep things light?"

Lucas, head and shoulders taller than Harper, nodded. "I suppose I'm used to hiking with a more experienced group," he said with a grin.

Milly bit her lower lip, holding back an angry retort. No doubt Lucas's crack was aimed at her. *The guy's a gym junkie, probably short on brain cells*, she reminded herself. Still, his jibe hurt. Or maybe she just felt vulnerable and out of her comfort zone. The purpose of the trip was to heal some old wounds with her sister, she could certainly cope with a macho pig like Lucas.

She hefted her pack, sliding it across her back. "Don't slow down on my account," she nodded at Lucas. "I'm sure I can keep up."

"Keep up with what?" Judith asked from behind her.

"I was just telling Lucas we should slow down a bit," Harper answered. Milly noticed a look pass between them. Their eyes held for a second as if they both wanted to say more. *Have they been talking about me?* Milly knew Harper kept in touch with her sister, perhaps they'd become close. She felt a spark of resentment, mostly towards her sister. Harper had been Milly's friend since high school and now Judith had muscled in. *I'm being childish*, she told herself. What did it matter if they'd become friends? Milly tried to shrug it off but couldn't help feeling hurt. *It's like I'm an outsider. Harper could have told me they were friends.*

Judith tilted her chin and looked up at the sky. She seemed to be thinking. Milly followed her gaze. A cluster of clouds the colour of washed-out bed sheets hung overhead.

"We've got some climbing to do," Judith said, still staring at the sky. "We need to get a move on. If it rains, the rocks will be too slippery."

The thought of scaling a craggy cliff in the rain got Milly moving. The last thing she wanted was to slip and fall. She secured her shoulder straps, hoisting the weight of the pack up and waited while her sister did the same.

"Hang on," Harper said and ducked behind Milly. "Your pack's open."

Milly felt her friend tug on the straps. "You don't have to prove anything," she whispered. Milly felt her friend's breath on the side of her neck.

"I know," Milly answered under her breath.

Twenty minutes later, the trail petered out. Underfoot, dusty ground became hard and tightly packed. Patches of grit were punctuated by slabs of granite, where deceptively sharp bushes sprouted seemingly from every crevice. The landscape in this part of the Leeuwin-Naturaliste National Park became wild and austere. Milly hoped the rest of the hike would take them into more appealing terrain. The thought of spending two nights in this setting made her throat tighten and her stomach twist.

"We're right on top of the overhang," Lucas stopped and turned to face the women. There was no mistaking the excitement in his voice. "I'll get the ropes rigged up. If you wanna look over the edge." He pointed to the rocks about ten metres ahead. "Be careful, erosion can make some sections … unpredictable." He crouched beside his pack and began pulling out rope and rigging.

Judith and Harper seemed unfazed by Lucas's warning. Both were moving towards the rocks.

"Um, should we really be climbing on rocks that are eroding?" Milly raised her voice. Harper stopped walking and turned, but Judith continued to make her way towards the edge. "There's no trail here. It doesn't seem like climbers regularly use this area." Cold streams of sweat ran down her spine.

"It's fine as long as you know what you're doing," Lucas tipped his black baseball cap back on his head. Strands of dark hair clung to his forehead. "I've climbed in areas like this before and…"

"You haven't climbed this particular rock before?" Milly's voice ratcheted up another notch. Now Judith turned and regarded her with a grim expression.

Milly couldn't believe she was the only one who seemed concerned. She thought she saw Judith and Harper exchange a glance and wondered if they were worried about the prospect of climbing down a crumbling cliff *or* the look was about her reaction.

Lucas dropped the ropes and stood. "It's safe, I promise." The sky above him looked grey and ominous, but his voice sounded warm, earnest.

The change in his demeanour caught her off guard and Milly found herself wondering if she'd been too quick to judge him. Was she really afraid of the climb or had seeing Judith standing on the edge of the drop brought back images?

"Look," he said stepping towards her. "It's a safe climb. Only about twelve or so metres. I've done this sort of thing hundreds of times." He reached out and touched her shoulder. She could feel the warmth of his hand through her shirt. "You'll be fine."

"I'll go first," Judith said, and Milly realised she was standing beside her. "You'll be surprised how easy it is." She thought she heard kindness in her sister's voice.

"Okay," Milly nodded and let out a long breath. How could she refuse?

Geared up, Milly watched her sister step backwards over the edge. She had to admire her courage, Judith didn't even hesitate. She steadied herself and then nodded to Lucas who let loose some slack on the ropes. With a smooth hop and a small patter of tiny rocks, Judith began her descent.

From her vantage point on the ledge, Milly could see the endless expanse of bush and forest below. Silver gums, bush grasses, and tall marri trees grew in tightly-packed gatherings. Here and there, clusters of pines dotted the forest. Not native to these area, the shaggy trees seemed to take root wherever they could find soil. The array of trees variegated to form a breathtakingly rugged vista. The landscape below certainly held more appeal than the windswept heathland they'd travelled so far. Milly thought she saw glimpses of water in the distance and wondered if they'd be camping near a lake.

"Okay." Lucas pulled the rope back up the cliff. "You next." He turned to Milly.

Milly looked down. Judith nodded up to her. "It's a piece of cake. You'll be fine."

Milly considered herself to be reasonably fit. She tried to get to the gym at least once a week to work out or swim in the pool. Up until recently, she'd managed to go for a run before work sometimes. Nothing major, just fifteen minutes or so. Exercising kept her mind clear, helped her find focus when the memories threatened to swallow her up. Abseiling down a small ledge should be easy, yet her legs were trembling and her breathing laboured.

"Are you okay?" Harper asked, her brows drawn together. "If you can't manage it, we'll find another way." She looked at Lucas for support. "Maybe this isn't a good idea." Harper's tone sounded strained as if her words carried an undercurrent.

"If we head south, we can make our way down. The descent is rocky and steep, but no climbing required." He shrugged. "We won't get there before nightfall so we'll have to make camp up here somewhere."

Milly scanned the area. Clusters of green saltbushes with needle-like leaves dotted the rocky landscape. She couldn't ask everyone to spend the night in this area, not just because she was afraid of a little rock climbing.

"What's going on up there?" Judith sounded impatient.

"No. I'm fine," Milly kept her tone even, and tried for a smile. "Just a momentary bout of vertigo."

"Are you sure?" Harper sounded unconvinced.

"Yes. I'm looking forward to getting down there." She hesitated. "It looks amazing."

"Great. Let's get you rigged up." Lucas rattled the climbing gear.

"Uh," Milly pointed to their packs. "What about our stuff?"

"I'll lower them once you're down." The kindness she'd heard in his voice earlier had vanished and now he sounded irritated. She couldn't blame him, she probably seemed like a real prima donna.

"Can you lower my pack before I go down? There's things in there I really need." She eyed her blue nylon backpack. "Maybe I could wear it while I go down?"

Lucas put his hands on his hips and let out a long breath. "First you're too scared to climb and now you want to do it wearing your pack." His broad muscular shoulders slumped. "Why don't you…"

"We'll just lower it first." Harper snatched up the pack and shoved it into Lucas's hands. A look passed between them and then he nodded.

Maybe there was something going on between them? Her musings quickly vanished as Lucas lowered her pack and then harnessed her up for the drop. His fingers expertly working the rigs. Milly focused on his face, bent so close she could smell his scent, musky and sharp.

"Right," Lucas gave her a nod.

She crouched slightly and stepped back. A flurry of ripples filled her stomach and her breath came in bursts. Behind her, cool air slapped her shoulders. For a second, she thought she would somersault backwards and spin into thin air, but her feet found purchase on the rocks and she lowered herself away from the ledge.

"That's it," she could hear Lucas's voice from above. "Just take it slow, one step at a time."

She wanted to look up and find his face, use it to anchor herself to the world, but her chin wobbled on her neck so she kept her eyes straight ahead fixed on the grey stone, focusing on the cracks and swirls that decorated the ancient crag. Another step down. A shower of tiny stones and bits of rubble skittered past her head. Her shoes scraped the rock, almost sliding away from the surface of the cliff before securing themselves on an outcrop. She wondered why they weren't wearing helmets. *I'm sure people wear helmets when they do this kind of thing.*

Milly's breathing began to even out. Stepping over the edge had to be the hardest part; at least that was behind her. Within minutes her feet would be on the ground. A tiny flicker of pleasure blossomed in her chest. She'd let herself get worked up when it really wasn't that bad. The feel of the breeze against her back and the freedom of leaning back from the rocks felt almost exhilarating.

"Milly don't mo…" Harper's voice loud and urgent.

Milly's head snapped up. Lucas eyes were wide. Harper above him, her hand over her mouth. Milly realised something was wrong only a fraction of a second before the world dropped out from under her.

She heard herself shriek and her hiking boots thumping rock. Her body seemed to dip backwards and greyish blue filled her vision. A high-pitched scream cut through the air and then blackness.

Chapter Five

12 November, 2006
"Come on, Judith," Milly's excited voice echoed in the darkness. She looked over her shoulder to where her little sister scampered over the rocks.

"I don't know why I let her come." She grabbed Drew's arm and urged him on towards the top of the Reach.

The full moon decorated the rocks with silver light, every surface was shiny and enticing in the dark. Below, the river swirled, black as oil in the night. Milly ran her fingers up Drew's bare arm, his skin smooth and taunt over young muscle.

"You okay?" Drew pulled back and turned to Judith. His arm slipped out of Milly's grasp and she watched in frustration as he reached his hand out and helped her sister to the top of the cliff.

Why had Mum insisted she bring Judith along? It was meant to be a party for older kids yet, as usual, Milly was saddled with her seventeen-year-old sister. In the distance, the sound of traffic hummed, but on Blackwell Reach the streets and houses seemed miles away.

Milly held the six pack of beer above her head. The cans were already growing warm in the humid air. "Let's have a drink and watch the lights."

The rocky cliff looked over South Fremantle and the Swan River. The overhang jutted out ten metres above the water where ancient slabs of rock lurked below the surface. The Reach, a breath-taking and dangerous place, made Milly's blood pound in her ears. She wished she could've shown it to Drew without her sister tagging along.

"Why don't you go back down and sit on the beach with Harper?" Judith's constant presence grated on her nerves. She wanted to enjoy something really special with Drew, but her anger towards her sister soured the moment.

"I'll go if you want," Judith's heart-shaped face glowed in the silvery moonlight. Her soft full lips turned down in disappointment.

Milly felt a pang of guilt, though not enough to ask her to stay. She flopped down on a wedge-shaped rock, her short dress hitched up around her thighs, and waited for Drew to join her.

"It's okay," Drew said, taking Judith's hand. "Stay with us."

Oh great, Milly rolled her eyes and snapped a can of beer off the six pack. The sound of music and laughter drifted up from the beach below. *I may as well give up*, she thought, watching Drew fawn over her sister. She popped the can open and chugged its contents, almost gagging in the process.

"Let's leap off the Reach," she laughed in the darkness, her voice sounded hollow as if it were coming from inside a cave. Once the words were out, Milly liked the idea. She tossed the can over her shoulder and heard it bounce against the rocks with a tiny clang. "Yeah, we can strip down to our underwear and go for it." She tore another can off the dwindling six pack and opened it. The smell made her stomach churn, but she forced herself to take a sip.

"I like the sound of the stripping," Drew chuckled and pulled a can off the pack.

He sat down beside Milly, his thigh pressing against her exposed leg. She felt a little bubble of excitement spark low in her belly. Drew's dark eyes glittered with mischief in the moonlight. He leaned forward and popped his can, then put it to his lips. Milly watched his throat work as he swallowed. There was something about him, his movements were languid and sexy. His voice deep, almost throaty. Yet he seemed kind and unaware of his own attractiveness. Usually cool and unimpressed by guys her own age, she found herself eager to impress him.

"You know you're hopeless with heights. As if you'd jump from up here." Judith said reaching for the beers.

"No way." Milly slapped her sister's hand. "Not for you. Mum would kill me if I let you drink." She glanced at Drew who seemed uninterested in the girl's exchange. "I haven't been afraid of heights since I was twelve."

Judith laughed, a teasing sound. "Oh yeah, you're the least adventurous person I know. You get nervous in lifts."

Drew chuckled and Milly could feel the heat rushing to her face. She hoped the full moon didn't expose her embarrassment. A high-pitched laugh rose up from the beach. Even though she knew the party was too far away for anyone to have heard Judith's remarks, Milly suddenly felt as if everyone were laughing at her.

"You're such a baby, Judith. The only people you know are in high school. Why don't you go down to the beach and stop hanging around?" Even in the moonlight she could see the hurt on her sister's face, but she seemed unable to stop herself. "You're an embarrassment." The last words came out with a harshness she didn't know she possessed.

"Okay," Drew blew out a long breath. "I think the three of us should go back down. It's getting late." He stood over Milly and took her arm.

She could feel tears building in her eyes. She'd made a fool of herself in front of him and worse, she'd acted like a bitch to Judith. Her stomach lurched and a stream of vomit shot out of her mouth splashing the rocks at Drew's feet.

"Oh God," she moaned and put her head on her knee.

"It's okay," Drew's voice sounded soft near her ear. "Let's get you back to the beach." He took hold of her upper arm and helped her to her feet.

"I'll meet you down there."

"What?" Drew released her arm and turned.

Milly staggered to her left, but caught herself before she lost her footing. Confused, she looked over Drew's shoulder. Her mouth dropped open and a puff of vomit-laced breath burst out. Judith stood in her bra and pants at the edge of the Reach, her white skin almost glowing in the moonlight. On the rocks at her feet, her discarded party dress looked like a puddle.

Drew stepped towards Judith, his arms outstretched. "Don't." His plea mingled with Milly's "No" to form an indiscernible roar.

Milly grabbed Drew's shoulder and tried to push past him. Her sandals skittered over the rocks; she was vaguely aware of his shirt ripping. Before either of the two could reach her, Judith let out a yelp and plunged into the darkness.

Milly's throat closed like a fist. She tried to call her sister's name, but her words were swallowed by panic. From below, the sound of flesh slapping water and a cheer of mingled voices from the party. Milly shook her head trying to block the image of her sister leaping over the cliff from her mind.

* * *

"Milly? Milly, answer me."

Her eyelids pulsed as if a blinding light were trying to push its way through them into her brain. The smell of wet leaves and something coppery filled her nose and mouth. A cold shock against her cheek sent a jolt through her body.

"Please, open your eyes," Judith's voice, hoarse and frightened brought her to the surface of consciousness.

Milly blinked and a bolt of pain like a shaft of iron pierced her head. Her eyes opened and Judith's face hovered over her. "Thank God. I thought I'd lost you." Judith's warm breath assaulted her skin. "You stopped breathing. I thought … I didn't think you'd come back."

Over Judith's shoulder, orange light melted the grey sky. The outline of the cliff cut a jagged finger across the firmament.

Chapter Six

Milly moved her head, trying to sit up, but Judith pushed her back down. "Don't move, something might be broken."

"Broken?" Milly repeated the word, her lips felt sloppy and wet. "Did I? What …" her voice trailed off. Her thoughts were muddy. She wanted to ask her what happened. "Where's Drew?" The moment the words were out, she remembered. The images came in snatches and then winked on and off.

"You know where Drew is," Judith's tone changed from relieved to hesitant, wary. "He's been dead for ten years."

She knew that. *Why did I ask about him?* The back of her head screamed with pain and her whole scalp prickled. She let out a moan and winced. The movement of her mouth aggravated the pain.

"You had a bad fall," Judith began. "I don't know what happened, something with the ropes."

"Harper?" Milly asked and tried to raise her hands to her face. A shock of agony seared through her lower back. The pain was so unexpected she tipped her head back and cried out. The movement set off another wave of scalp-raising torture at the back of her head.

"For God's sake, Milly stop moving," Judith's voice trembled, the last word a wail. "You're hurt. I don't know how badly, but you have to keep still." She took a deep breath. "Harper couldn't get a signal on her phone so she and Lucas are hiking back to the beach to get help."

The image of Lucas's face leaning over the cliff flashed in Milly's mind. The last few seconds before she fell became clearer. She tried to push through the pain in her head and remember exactly what happened. Everything seemed out of kilter, off somehow. One minute she'd been harnessed up, descending the rock face, the next flat on her back, her scalp on fire with agony.

"How did I fall?" she managed through clenched jaw.

Judith's face moved out of view. Milly almost turned her head to see what she was doing, but remembered the pain from a few moments ago, and stared up at the vermillion sky instead.

"I'm not sure what happened," Judith sounded uncertain. "You were managing the descent really well and then," she let out a shuddering breath. "You just fell – hard."

Milly moved her right hand, unsure what to expect. Mercifully, the movement was pain free. She touched her fingers to her face, they came away wet. Afraid to move her head, she held them above her eyes. Her hand, stained red, trembled. She licked her lips and the rusty taste of blood filled her mouth.

"It's okay." Judith's voice from her left. "I think you bit your bottom lip when you landed. It's not too bad."

"Can I have a sip of water?" Her throat felt coated in blood, the taste sickening.

"Good thing Lucas lowered your pack down or we wouldn't even have water." Milly heard nylon rustling and Judith's face reappeared above her.

"I don't know how we're going to do this without choking you." Judith held the bottle near her chin.

"I'll try and sit up." Milly didn't relish the thought of moving her head, but the need to clear the foul taste from her mouth seemed more urgent than staving off the pain.

"No." Judith put her hand on Milly's chest. "What if you've injured your spine?"

Milly thought for a moment and considered her body in its entirety. She could feel the cold air on her legs and move her feet, the pain in her back was brutally evident, but mostly on the left. There came a pulsing from the back of her head and her lip stung. She felt no pain in her neck.

"I don't think so. It's just my head and my lower back, more towards my left side." *Why aren't I in the recovery position?* The thought only fleeting and easily dismissed. *Judith was probably too scared to move me.*

With her thoughts clearing and an assessment of her injuries complete, Milly raised her head. Splotches of red swam in her eyes and jolts of pain threaded her skull.

"Slowly," Judith cautioned, sliding her hand under Milly's shoulders.

With a groan, she raised herself up and to the right, resting on her arm. Her vision wavered, the splotches danced. Her stomach clenched but she managed to push back a surge of nausea. She wondered if this was how Drew had felt. *Did he have time to feel anything?* Her mind kept skipping back in time, throwing up images and questions.

Judith pressed the bottle to Milly's lips and tipped it for her to drink. Water mingled with blood washed her throat.

"Better?"

"Mm." Sitting up felt more comfortable and took the pressure off the back of her head. Her vision cleared and she began to take note of their surroundings.

The orange-tinted sky turned grey as the light died. They were in a clearing of sorts, about three metres out from the rock face. Sandy soil with patches of bush grass sprouting wherever they could take root. Tall marri trees and shaggy natives edged the small area. The thought of being amongst the trees at night sent a shiver of panic up Milly's spine.

"Cold?" Judith asked.

Milly realised she was shivering. "Yeah, a bit. What time is it?"

Judith stowed the bottle in Milly's pack and took off her hat. "I don't know. I'm not wearing a watch."

"When will they be back?" She hesitated, "I know you don't know exactly, but how long have they been gone?"

"I told you I'm not wearing a watch." Judith stood over the pack with her back to Milly. "I don't know how long they'll be … As long as it takes them I suppose." Judith rolled her sleeves down and fastened them at her wrists. "I'm going to build a fire. I know we're not supposed to start fires out here, but I'm not letting us freeze. Besides," she turned and regarded her sister. "You might be in shock."

Still propped up on her elbow, Milly watched Judith gather sticks and leaves. In the gloom she looked ghostly, a shadowy figure moving amongst the trees. Milly swallowed back another wave of nausea and pulled herself upwards by digging her fingers into the soft ground and shuffling her butt.

A spark of pain turned like a screw driven into the back of her skull. She gasped and clutched the side of her head. Slowly, she worked her fingers backwards until they were buried in her short dark hair. She found an area that felt like a baseball sized watery blister and torn skin sticky with blood. She applied slight pressure to the swelling and winced. Around her, the wind stirred the trees, rattling their branches.

"Okay, that's a start." Judith's arms were piled high with sticks and dry branches. "I think we should move nearer the rock face. It'll offer *some* protection from the weather."

Judith dumped her load close to the rocks and turned to her sister. "How's your head?"

"A bit better."

Judith nodded and squatted on the ground to build a fire. "When I've finished here, I'll get your sleeping bag. The cliff will block the wind so we should be warm enough."

Milly reached around with her left hand. Her fingers found a damp spot on her shirt. The muscle beneath her hand felt bruised and swollen. Even the slightest pressure caused a flash of pain. Another wave of nausea rose up, it took all her willpower to force it down.

"Can you help me?" She'd forgotten about her watch. The black leather strap looked embedded in her wrist. "I need to get my watch off; I think it's cutting off the circulation."

"Just a sec," Judith continued arranging the sticks in a small tepee shape.

"Please, Judith. It really hurts." Milly hated the demanding tone in her voice, but couldn't understand why her sister seemed unwilling to keep still. Almost from the moment Milly had opened her eyes, Judith had been rushing around looking for things to do.

"Yes. Sorry. Let me help you." Judith came over and dropped to her knees next to Milly. "Sorry, Mil. I just want to make sure you're warm and comfortable." Milly ignored the reproach in her sister's voice and focused on what Judith had called her. *Mil*.

Growing up, she'd called Judith *Jude* and in return, her sister called her *Mil*. They'd both made no secret of how much they hated their old-fashioned names. But their mother, a writer of historical romances, would hear none of it.

"Millicent and Judith are elegant, timeless names. You'll thank me when you're older." Milly could almost hear her mother's voice.

Memories of her mum were all she had now, and even those seemed like a dream swallowed by the endless march of time. Memories were meaningless unless shared with a fellow time traveller.

"Do you remember what Mum used to say about our names?"

Judith continued to work on the watch strap with gentle fingers. "How can I forget?" She gave a soft laugh and glanced up at her sister. The dying light made it difficult to see her face, but Milly thought she was smiling.

"You'll thank me when you're older," both women said in unison.

They laughed. Milly shrieked and touched the back of her head which only made Judith laugh harder. *Maybe there is a future for us*, Milly thought even as her head throbbed.

A piercing howl tore through the dusk. An unmistakable sound of pain mixed with terror. Above the cliff the wind moaned. In the nearby trees a flock of birds took flight, their panicked cries blocking out all other sound.

"Holy fuck." Judith gripped her sister's wrist, her pupils dilated into huge black discs. Milly let out a cry of pain. "Sorry." Judith's words came out in a breathless whisper. "What was that?"

"I don't know." Milly whispered back, her right hand clamped to her injured back. "Get the fire going. I don't want to be sitting here in the dark."

Another howl pierced the air, this one closer. It echoed overhead, a scream rising as if it would go on forever and then abruptly cut off.

Chapter Seven

Harper's hiking boots thumped across the rocks. Her chest heaved as panicky gasps replaced regular breathing. She could hear him behind her, footfalls thundering through the dirt. Her eyes darted in every direction, searching for an avenue of escape. She didn't dare waste precious seconds looking back.

The craggy stretch of rocks ended with a metre or so drop. She made the split-second decision to leap forward and hope she could land on her feet and keep going. There was still enough light by which to make out the approaching drop, but it was dying fast. If she hesitated, he'd be on top of her.

The rocks disappeared as she leaped forward, arms circling outwards to increase her momentum, ponytail flying over her head. For an instant, she hung in the air and then her boots struck the ground with enough force to jar her knees and send her careening forward at breakneck speed. Her right leg buckled and she spilled over, arms outstretched.

Her hands hit the tightly-packed dirt and she heard a brittle snap, loud and sickening in the twilight's silence. A shaft of agony tore up her right arm. Her head snapped back and a howl, heavy with pain and fear, escaped her lips.

Behind her, his boots smacked over the rocks. She had no choice but to keep moving. Harper choked out a sob and staggered to her feet. The agony in her arm apparent, but swallowed by adrenalin. If she could make it to the trees, she might be able to hide.

Instinctively, she clutched her injured arm to her body. The trees were less than a few metres away, draped in shadows. The temperature dipped, chilling the sweat on Harper's terrified face. She sprinted forward, her shirt ballooning out behind her like a cape. His hand closed over the fabric and he jerked her backwards.

"No!" It came out as strangled gasp.

Harper lowered her head and bent her knees, tipping her body forward she ploughed away from him with strength she didn't know she possessed. The sound of fabric tearing, followed by a grunt, reminded her of a bull blowing air out of its nostrils. She broke free, stumbled to the right and then darted left.

The change of direction gave her the precious seconds she needed to make it to the trees. Behind her came panting and the crackle of branches snapping. It sounded like a wild animal breaking through the trees. She snatched another backward glance and saw a glint of dying light reflect off the blade of his knife. *I won't die like this. Not hunted like an animal.* She willed herself to find the strength and speed to outrun him.

Harper cut to the right and rounded a peppermint tree. Then came what might be her only chance. A startled yelp and snapping branches. She looked back and he was on the ground, his face hidden by the growing darkness. His fall would give her a few seconds to lose him. If she could find a place to hide, maybe a weapon, she might have a chance.

Please, God – she mouthed a silent prayer and plunged deeper into the bush ignoring the needle-like leaves that tore at her arms. A fallen tree swathed in dead branches and dry leaves offered a possible hiding place. Harper scampered over the trunk. Her right foot slid out from under her. She came down on her injured arm. She heard a stomach-turning rip, like the sound of a threadbare sheet being torn apart. Her back arched and a primal scream erupted from her bloodless lips.

She slapped her left hand over her mouth in an effort to silence herself. Tears and mucus covered her face. She listened and held back the hiccupping breaths building in her chest. *Where is he? What's he waiting for?*

Hide or keep going? She had maybe two seconds to make the choice that would see her live or die. She pushed on.

Ten metres farther, Harper veered left and spotted a mass of grass trees. There were at least four in a cluster. One had died or been knocked over by an animal, its usually black stump looked grey in the near darkness. If she could make her way in between the short, squat trees, the fallen stump might act as a barrier and block her from view. Around her, the bush sat in silence save the singing of insects. She fell to her knees and half-crawled, half-dragged herself behind the grass trees.

She held her injured arm against her belly and cupped her left hand over her mouth to silence her laboured breathing. Inside the copse of trees, she sat in almost total darkness. A crackle of leaves from the left – it had to be him. She could almost smell his musky odour. A rustle, as if a branch had been carefully moved. She could hear the blood beating in her ears. *My beautiful Judith*, she thought and closed her eyes.

Chapter Eight

"What should we do?" Judith flicked her lighter, but the flame refused to catch.

"Get that fire going then toss me my pack. I've got a torch." Milly looked around, her eyes darting in all directions.

Darkness fell, enveloping everything around them. They'd soon be blanketed by night. The shadows between the trees spread and stretched until it became impossible to discern where the branches ended and the night began. The only sound, the clicking of Judith's lighter and the constant buzz of insects.

"Got it."

The fire took hold. Milly watched Judith lean forward, tossing handfuls of dry leaves into the flames, then bundling sticks on top of the incipient fire. As she worked, she kept glancing up at Milly as if checking her sister hadn't vanished. The glow of the fire threw a shimmering shadow upon the rock face, reflecting back and casting an arc of reassuring light.

Milly turned her head and scanned the darkness. She wondered if someone might be watching them from the shadows. If so, it would be impossible to tell. Using her hand to push off the ground, Milly struggled to her feet. The world shifted and she staggered to the left.

"What are you doing?" Judith rushed to her side. "You should have waited for me."

"I'm fine." She touched her hand to her head just to reassure herself that it wasn't spinning off her shoulders. "We should sit with our backs against the rock, that way we can see if …" She let her words trail off.

With Judith's hand on her back, Milly made her way around the fire and lowered herself against the rock face. She lifted her hand into her lap and frowned. Something hovered on the edge of her thoughts, but flew out of her mind before she could latch onto it.

Judith picked up the blue nylon pack and dropped it near the fire. She folded herself into a sitting position and began rummaging through the contents.

"It's in the front compartment," Milly offered, anxious to stop her sister searching her pack.

Judith opened the zip and fished out the small metal torch. She held it, but didn't turn it on. Milly could see her sister's body tremble. She wondered if it was caused by the plummeting temperature or fear.

"Who do you think made those noises?" Judith asked, turning to look at her sister. The firelight reflected in her eyes, lighting her face up with a yellowish glow. The question had been at the forefront of Milly's mind.

"I don't know." Milly gave a one-shouldered shrug. "Maybe another hiker, stuck out here like us?" Even as she said it, she knew it sounded lame.

Judith pulled the pack over and sat next to her. "You don't really believe that, do you?"

"I don't know what to think to be honest." Milly touched the back of her head. "I'm having trouble keeping everything straight."

Judith nodded and unclipped Milly's sleeping bag from the bottom of the pack. "Here, we can put this over us. It'll help with the cold."

Milly used her right hand to pull the sleeping bag up to her chin. "They should be back at the carpark by now, surely their phones work there?"

Judith nodded but made no comment. Nothing about the situation seemed right. Milly tried to convince herself her thinking was still muddled, but she couldn't help feeling she might be missing something.

"Where's my watch?" She remembered asking Judith to help her take it off before the screaming started.

"I don't know." Judith kept her gaze on the fire. "I must have dropped it when we heard the scream. It was definitely a woman. The screaming ... It sounded like a woman, don't you think?"

Her change of direction threw Milly for a second. "I ... Yes, I think so." She bit her bottom lip then winced as the cut there stung and opened up again. "What are you thinking?" She knew the answer even as she asked.

Judith dragged her eyes away from the fire. "Do you think it was Harper?" Her voice cracked, and Milly could see her sister's cheeks were wet.

Milly reached for her hand under the sleeping bag. It felt icy. "Anything could be happening. We don't know it was Harper screaming." There was so much she wanted to say. So many things she needed to tell her, but now wasn't the time.

"What's that?" Judith jumped and squeezed her hand tight enough to cut off the circulation. "In the trees, I... I thought I heard something."

Milly followed her sister's gaze. Three metres beyond the fire lay only blackness. It was impossible to see anything, human or animal. Suddenly Milly wondered if the fire was a good idea. If there was someone out there, the light would make the two women clearly visible to anyone watching. They'd be easy targets. *Targets for what?* Her mind raced in a dozen half-formed directions, all of them ominous. She shuddered and leaned against her sister.

"I don't hear anything," Milly whispered. "Maybe it's an animal. A kangaroo or something."

"Maybe," Judith drew out the word and swivelled her head in all directions. "Have you got anything in your pack we could use as a weapon?"

Milly hesitated, "I'm not …" She went over the inventory in her head. "Yes. There's a penknife. It's not very big. I bought it at the camping shop where I got the pack. It seemed like the sort of thing you need when you're camping." She gave a weak laugh.

Judith pushed down the sleeping bag and began rummaging through the pack. She pulled out several packets of jerky and a few energy bars. "Good, we should eat something." She tossed Milly a bar and kept searching. "What's this?" She pulled out a small plastic bottle of pills. And held it up in front of the fire. "Sothem?"

"That's just something the doctor prescribed."

Judith turned the bottle over in her hand and then looked at Milly with raised eyebrows. The silence stretched. Milly felt the need to explain, but now wasn't the time. "It's nothing." She tried to make her tone flippant, instead it came out harsh.

Judith shrugged and stuffed the bottle back in the pack. "And this?" She asked, pulling out a hip flask.

The thumping in the back of Milly's head ratcheted up a notch. *What are we doing?* There was something terrifying going on in the dark but Judith seemed more concerned with quizzing her on the contents of her pack.

"Jesus, Jude. Just find the knife and stop worrying about what I've got in my pack." This time, she didn't care if her tone sounded harsh; she wanted this whole thing to be over. She felt tears burning her eyes and bit her lip. "Shit," she winced and reached for the flask.

To her surprise, Judith softened. "Okay, Mil. Here." She unscrewed the top off the flask and put it in Milly's hand.

She held the flask in front of her and noticed her hand shaking. There were dark stains on her fingers; blood from her head and lip. Milly wrinkled her nose and took a sip from the hip flask. The bitter taste of vodka burned her throat. She grimaced, put the flask to her swollen bottom lip and took another hit. The alcohol left a pleasant trail of heat in her chest. She sniffed and wiped her tears away on the back of her hand.

"Found it," Jude held up the penknife and pulled out the blade. The ten-centimetre shaft glinted in the firelight. "God, Mil, what did you think we'd be doing out here? Skinning rabbits?"

A wave of drowsiness washed over her, Milly wondered briefly if drinking vodka with a head injury was a good idea. But before any concrete concerns were formed, her thoughts flittered away. The smell of damp leaves and burning wood invaded her nostrils. She blinked her eyes and tried to focus on the fire. Judith's voice hummed in her ears. She knew her sister was speaking, but the buzzing blocked out her words. Staying awake seemed important, but she couldn't remember why.

She had the impression someone was calling her. The voice soft and familiar. Her limbs felt weighted as if anchored down. Part of her mind kept pulling her back to consciousness while painless sleep beckoned. The fire seemed to turn sideways then wink out.

Chapter Nine

12 November, 2006
Milly stumbled to the edge of the Reach and fell to her knees. The water, black and churning, looked distant and wild, streaked silver by the full moon. She scoured the surface for any sign of her sister. They were close to the mouth of the river and the wind, driven in from the Indian Ocean, welled up and whipped her hair around her face.

"Jude. Jude!" The name turned into a scream as the seconds passed and her sister failed to surface.

Below, the laughter faded and ended with a spate of claps. Seconds piled up and time stretched. Milly leaned forward, straining as far as gravity would allow. Ribbons of white water frothed against slabs of rock jutting in clusters to the left of the Reach. *Did she hit water or rock?* Milly's frantic mind hurdled from one terrifying thought to the next.

"Jude? Judith?" Milly's voice broke.

She pushed herself up and stepped to the edge. She couldn't waste any more time. She had no choice but to jump. In the time it would take for her to climb down and get to the beach, Judith would drown. Far out to the left, she could see two figures wading into the water. They'd have to swim twenty metres out and then around the rocks in order to reach the patch of deep water directly below the cliff.

"What are you doing?" Drew's voice cut through her panic. "You'll kill yourself." He took hold of her arm.

Milly's mouth opened, she searched his face without really seeing him. Judith had been in the water at least a minute and a half. There was no time to argue.

She looked back at the water. It seemed to be shrinking farther and farther away. The Reach growing higher by the second. Milly's stomach lurched, an icy sensation gripped her legs. In the seconds between making the decision to jump and Drew stopping her, the fear of heights that plagued her all her life, reared up.

"Drew," she grabbed at his shoulder. "Do something. She'll die."

They held on to each other, Milly shivering with panic, and Drew's face devoid of colour. Indecision and fear in his wide, dark eyes.

"Jump, Drew. For God's sake, you have to do something."

His mouth opened as if he were about to say something. Then he was gone. He plummeted through the moonlight, his body twisting at a ninety-degree angle and his arms grabbing at air. He hit the water to the left of the Reach, not with a splash but a smacking sound that reminded Milly of a wet towel hitting concrete.

She could feel a scream building in her throat, it stuck as if blocked by a solid mass. Drew's body jerked sideways by the tide and then slipped from the rock he'd landed on and disappeared into the black churning waters of the Swan River.

As the young man's form slipped beneath the water, another shape broke the surface a few metres away. Judith's head bobbed up and her hair whipped back, a trail of droplets flew like pearls in the moonlight.

"Ha," she yelped, her voice echoing off the walls of the Reach. "Not such a baby now, am I?"

Milly plunged her hands into her hair and rocked back. Her legs seemed to collapse under her as her butt hit the rocks. Next to her, Judith's dress fluttered and rolled across the rocky outcrop. She could hear screaming coming from below. Voices raised in panic. Milly tilted her head and looked up at the stars. The night sky over Fremantle was an endless blanket of blackness.

"Milly. What happened?" Harper's voice startled her. "I was on my way up when I heard the screaming. Where's Judith and Drew?"

Milly kept her eyes on the stars and raised her hand, one finger pointing towards the edge of the Reach.

Chapter Ten

Milly jerked and tried to swat at her face. The movement sent tendrils of pain through her head and a whip-crack of agony across her left wrist. There was no feeling in her right arm. She blinked, her eyes felt sticky with grit and her tongue plastered to the roof of her mouth. The sound of magpies warbling assaulted her ears.

The fire had burned down to nothing more than a pile of ashes with a wisp of smoke rising lazily in the pale grey light. Milly tried to sit up, but her right arm remained pinned under her weight, refusing to move. She rolled onto her back; above her the jagged outline of the cliff blocked the sky. Her recollection of the previous night was cloudy. She had no idea if she'd passed out or fallen asleep. *Where's Judith?*

Still huddled under the sleeping bag, she worked her right hand into a fist, opening and closing it trying to force the useless limb back to life. Pins and needles danced up her arm as the feeling gradually returned. She pushed herself into a sitting position and looked around.

She spotted her sister slumped against the rock face, her head hidden by the hood of a black fleecy jacket. The knife, still open, lay in her lap. Milly let out a long shuddering breath. For a moment, she'd feared Judith had left her in the wilds to fend for herself. Or worse, she'd been taken.

A chill seemed to rise from the ground beneath her, saturating her shorts and shirt with clingy dampness. The trees were blanketed in soft, smoky mist that floated between the trunks and curled around the branches. Milly realised she was seeing everything for the first time. Yesterday, after the fall, she'd been too dazed to take in her surroundings. When the screaming started, she'd been frightened, struggling to see in the dark. The morning light revealed the bleak beauty of the landscape as well as a feeling of isolation.

It seemed they were in a valley at the edge of a forest of sorts. She recalled looking down on the area from above. Lucas had said something about another way down, but her thoughts were still muddy. She snatched up her pack using her right hand to sift through the contents. She found the pill bottle at the bottom of her bag and managed to unscrew it using one hand. She'd dreamt of the Reach again last night. The images and sounds hauntingly clear in her mind. A knot of anxiety sat in the pit of her stomach. Something strange – dangerous even – was unfolding around her. She had to keep her nerves under control, if not for herself then for Judith's sake. She glanced over at her sister. Satisfied she was still asleep, she swallowed a tiny red pill dry and put the bottle back in the pack.

"You're up," Judith's voice, croaky with sleep, made her jump.

"Yes. Just thinking about coffee."

"How's your head?" Judith stretched her back and groaned. Her face was hidden under the shadow of the hood.

Milly touched her fingers to the back of her head where her hair lay matted over a large fluid-filled bubble. "Still sore. Did you hear any more screams?" she hesitated. "You know, after I …" Milly let her words trail off.

"You passed out, Mil." Judith's tone sounded flat, exhausted. "But to answer your question, no. No more screams, but I'm sure something was moving around out there." She gestured towards the trees. "I don't think we should stay here waiting any longer. I'm worried about that head injury. I know you had a few sips of vodka, but that doesn't explain why you passed out cold." She pushed the hood back. Her eyes were red-rimmed and puffy. "And I'm worried about Harper. If they made it back to the carpark, help would be here by now."

Milly wanted to argue, tell her she was overreacting, but she'd be lying and she'd done too much of that over the years. "You're right. We should go. Lucas said something about there being another way down here." Milly rubbed her palm across her forehead as if trying to force the memory.

Judith waited, her eyes trained on her sister. "It'll come to me," Milly said. She tried to focus on her last memories before she fell. She didn't want to climb down. She could almost hear Lucas's impatient, almost angry voice. It came to her. "No climbing required." She repeated his words aloud, nodding. "He said we could go south, it would take three hours and be steep, but no climbing."

"Alright," Judith stood. "I'll pack our stuff. We'll eat then move." She looked smaller draped in Milly's hoodie. Judith must have noticed her sister eyeing the jacket. "I got it out of your pack. Here." She pulled on the zip. "You should wear it, it's freezing."

"No. That's okay. I'll wear the track pants, you keep the jacket."

They ate protein bars washed down with sips of water. Not the tastiest breakfast Milly had ever had, but at least they were together. Together and speaking. Milly wondered if now might be a good time to start being honest with her sister. She waited until Judith had finished her last bite of food.

"About Mum's house." Her stomach did a strange flip flop. "I know you want to keep it, but…"

"Yes, I do. I tried to tell you that yesterday *and* in my email." Judith's tone hardened. "It would be nice if you would at least think about what I'm asking before you shut me down."

Their mother had made Milly executor of her estate. Maybe that was part of the problem. Judith resented her for what happened at the Reach; Milly accepted that, even though it had been Judith who caused the whole thing. *Not all of it was my fault,* she reminded herself.

Milly shook her head and a stab of pain blossomed at the back of her skull. "Just let me explain?"

"You don't need to." Judith stuffed the wrapper from her protein bar in the front pocket of her shorts. "Mum put you in charge. She never really trusted me after …" her words faltered. "After what happened. I've had to live with it. You ran away and I was the one everyone blamed." Judith pulled the knife out of her waistband and opened the blade.

Milly's eyes widened and her jaw fell open. She shuffled back on her bottom trying to put some distance between herself and the knife.

Judith frowned and her eyes moved between her sister and the knife in her hand. "Oh for God's sake, Milly." Judith's eyes widened in surprise. "You think I'd stab you?" her voice trembled. "What do you think I am?"

"No. No, I didn't think that." Milly's face felt hot. "I'm just…"

"Forget it." Judith's tone was thick with emotion. She shrugged off the jacket and untucked her shirt. She used the blade to cut a strip of fabric off the entire rim of the garment. She did the same again and then held the knife in her teeth while she tied the two strips together.

"Stand up," she ordered.

With her left side knotted in pain, Milly struggled to stand. Judith flung the strip of fabric over her shoulder and grabbed Milly under her arm.

"I saw this in a movie," Judith spoke around the handle of the knife. She took hold of the back of Milly's shirt and pulled it up around her chest. Milly gasped as the cold air hit her. "Sorry," Judith said and pressed the wadded-up strip of fabric to the wound. "Now hold it there," she instructed. "You've got a nasty gash on your side."

Milly did as she was told, realising what her sister had in mind. Judith laid the remaining strip of fabric across Milly's back. She wrapped the fabric around Milly's stomach and repeated the process, stepping around her sister and tying the makeshift bandage just above Milly's navel. When she finished, Milly's back and belly were tightly wrapped.

"I'd say you wrenched a muscle when you fell. With your lower back immobilised, it won't be as painful when we walk." Judith stood in front of her, tilting her chin to look up into her sister's face. Up close, Milly could see the fine lines that circled Judith's eyes. At twenty-seven, her sister looked drawn and solemn. Two years her senior, Milly wondered if the years of guilt had left her with similar signs of anguish.

"Thanks, Jude." Milly hesitated, "I lost my job." It wasn't how she'd rehearsed it in her mind, but the words were out and she felt relieved.

"What?" Judith drew her brows together, her mouth tightened.

"I haven't worked in nearly a year." Once she'd started, the words tumbled out. "I've been having problems. Problems at work and, and you know, just keeping things together. The pills you found, they're for anxiety and depression." Milly half-turned away and focused on the trees. The mist still hung in the air as if suspended by invisible hands. "That's why I wanted us to sell the house … I need the money."

She felt Judith's hand on her shoulder, but kept her eyes trained on the hazy forest. Her face burned and her heart rate quickened. *What am I doing?* Did she really want to start confessing her sins to Judith? Afraid of what she might say next, she bit on her injured lip and winced as the salty taste of blood filled her mouth.

"It's good you're being honest with me," Judith spoke softly as if dealing with someone unstable. "You can tell me the truth, whatever that may be."

Milly's head swung around. "What? What do you mean? I … I just told you why I wanted to sell the house. What more truth do you want?"

Judith's hand dropped from Milly's shoulder. She shrugged. "Nothing. I'm just glad you told me." She gave a brief smile. "Are you ready to go?"

Milly looked around the makeshift campsite, then up at the cliff. "Yeah. I'll just duck into the trees for a pee."

* * *

Judith watched Milly make her way into the trees. She seemed to be lurching to the right. Maybe the back pain was throwing her off balance, but Judith had a grim inkling the head injury was the problem. Since the fall, her sister had been behaving strangely. *What do I know? I haven't spoken to her in ten years.* Still, the sooner they were out of the National Park, the better. Babysitting Milly through a head injury had never been the plan.

How did things get so complicated? It started out as a simple idea; spend a few days alone with her sister. Sort things out, get to the truth. After ten years of secrets and lies had she really believed Milly would admit the truth? Judith wondered if Milly knew what the truth was. One thing was for sure, she'd made a mistake letting Lucas get involved.

He'd been so sure of himself, the expert on hiking and abseiling. The Leeuwin-Naturaliste National Park had been his idea. Judith rubbed her fingers over her eyes. She felt so damn tired. Last night after the screaming started, she'd been too scared to sleep. Everything had gone to hell and now Milly was hurt and Harper and Lucas were God knows where.

How did the idea go from a hiking trip to dropping her sister off a cliff? They'd talked the plan through, going round and round, but it always came back to the same thing – frighten Milly into spitting out what really happened at the Reach. Harper never liked the idea, but Lucas promised them nothing could go wrong. Judith made a clicking noise with her tongue. *What the fuck was I thinking?*

She picked up Milly's pack and swung it over her shoulders. Tilting her head, she regarded the cliff. What the hell had Lucas and Harper been thinking? They were supposed to drop Milly a few metres. Enough to scare her, instead they'd nearly killed her. Judith ran her fingers through her hair. The sickening thump when Milly hit the ground echoed in her mind. She closed her eyes and tried to block the sound and image.

She'd been angry with her sister for so long, she didn't think she had any other feelings left for her. But yesterday when she thought she'd lost her, it felt like being torn in two. And what about Harper? Judith turned around and strained her eyes trying to see through the trees. Something *had* happened, she could feel it in her bones. Harper would never leave her out here. Frightened and worried sick. The only other explanation didn't bear thinking about.

If something's happened to Harper, it'll be just like Drew: my fault. She'd lived with the guilt of Drew's death and somehow found a way to move on, mostly by blaming her sister. This time she would have to bear the guilt alone, and without Harper she couldn't see a future. Judith wondered what the hell they'd hoped to achieve by getting

Milly out here and frightening her. *The truth*. Wasn't that what all this was about?

"Judith," Milly's voice, shrill and panicked rang out.

Judith sprinted into the trees pushing branches and bushes aside, the pack bounced against her spine and scraped up and down her neck. A thin vapour still hung in the air, blurring the lines between foliage and ground. Her boot caught on something and she stumbled to the left, catching herself against the barrel-sized trunk of what might have been a gum tree.

"Judith!" Her sister's voice louder and to the right.

Judith jerked her head around, confused. The mist and dense forest caught the sound and played it back and forth making it difficult for her to pinpoint the origin of the call.

Judith cupped her hands around her mouth. "Where are you?"

A second later, Milly's voice felt clear enough to be almost next to her, "Here."

Judith turned towards the sound and rounded a snatch of bushes. Milly, eyes wide and track pants clutched at her waist, stood unmoving amongst the misty greenery. Her face, already bleached of colour from the head injury, looked ashen.

Judith stepped towards her, arms out ready to catch her if she went down, but something in her sister's face stopped her. Judith realised it wasn't pain, but fear etched into Milly's features. Turning her head, she followed Milly's gaze.

Judith sucked in a sharp breath and pressed a hand against her open mouth. Strung from a low-hanging branch less than a metre away, a shredded backpack turned lazily in the morning breeze. She reached out a hand and stilled the movement.

"It's Harper's." Milly's voice, little more than a whisper, dragged her attention away from the pack. "It's just like mine only black. She helped me pick it out."

"We need to move." Judith turned to her sister. "Now."

Chapter Eleven

The husk of a burnt-out gum tree offered shelter from the cold. He'd denied himself sleep, preferring to watch the night sky and listen. There'd been no trace of Blondie since she'd given him the slip, but that meant nothing. Out here he was the powerful one. Losing her had been an oversight, but not unrepairable.

Pale light cut through the trees and sent jagged streaks across the surrounding foliage. He breathed deeply, sucking in the crisp cool air. *It will be a good day. A day to turn things around.* He'd been the weak one once, frightened and terrorised but slowly he'd taken back the power. His mind drifted back to the old woman.

Finding her house had been simple. Once he made certain of Blondie's connection to Judith Birdsworth, locating Judith and Millicent's mother had been easier than he'd ever dreamed. The tricky part came when he tried to get inside. He thought of the manicured gardens of the huge house, and bitter tasting bile filled his mouth. He spat a glob of frothy liquid onto the blackened roots of the tree and absently trailed the toe of his boot through the mess.

He'd sat, much like he did now, in the gardens and watched the old lady. He remembered seeing her open the double glass doors – they had some fancy name but he couldn't think of it – and wander around near the sparkling pool. She was rich, he'd always known that, but until he saw the house, he hadn't really understood what that meant. A writer, that's what the old lady called herself. She wrote crappy romance stuff about the olden days. He'd tried to read one, but it was worse than the stuff they forced on him at school.

Above him, magpies sung as if announcing the dawn. His eyes, glassy with lack of sleep, watched a distant place only visible to him. He had patience, he'd proved that to himself time and again. Four times he'd sat in the old lady's garden, watching – waiting for her to leave the doors open. Sometimes he liked to think of himself as a snake; clever and watchful, slipping through the world unnoticed until he decided to strike.

The day he'd finally made it inside … his mind faltered. Her name, the old lady's, something old-fashioned like the sisters. He tapped his fingers on the rough bark of the tree. *Amy? No, Amelia. Yeah, that's it.* He said the name aloud, enjoying the way his voice rose when he hit the *a* at the end. Amelia Birdsworth. Poor old cow; his mind conjured up an image of the woman, standing at the top of the stairs. She'd been so surprised to find him behind her, it'd taken him only the slightest push to send her reeling down the stairs.

He recalled the way her mouth hung open like one of those clowns you drop balls in to. It really was funny. He chuckled and his fingers drummed faster against the tree. When she hit the stairs, her old bones started snapping like pretzels. By the time she rolled over and hit the tiled floor at the bottom, she wasn't a pretty sight.

Thinking about Amelia Birdsworth sent a shiver of excitement racing across his shoulders. After the fall, he'd crouched over her and watched her breathing. At one point, her eyes opened and she started to crow like an old chook. He leaned over her and sniffed. She'd pissed herself, he could smell it.

"When I'm done with you, I'm going to find your daughters and have a really good time with them." He whispered the words in her ear, letting his lips brush against her skin.

That really got her going. He chuckled at the memory. She managed to turn her head and look at him. *Man, if looks could kill. That old bird would have skinned me alive.* But she wasn't able to do anything by then but crow and gag. He felt almost sorry when she finally gave up and died. He wished he hadn't pushed her down the stairs. He should have taken his time and enjoyed it a bit more, but he couldn't risk being caught in the house when one of her old biddy friends came knocking.

She'd been the warm up; soon it would be time for the main event. He stuck his head out from inside the burnt-out tree. The air smelled of mossy rot and the forest looked spooky with mist. He settled back inside his hiding place and let out a contented sigh. He decided to wait a few more minutes, give the air a chance to warm up. There was no great hurry, still plenty of time to find Blondie and start the fun.

Chapter Twelve

The pain in her arm spiked sometime in the night. Harper risked lying on her side, her knees drawn up close to her chin. Thirst and hunger clawed at her insides making every moment torture. Inside the crop of grass trees, thin streaks of grey light climbed over her body. She'd slept, or at least she thought she had. The night, endless and black, was finally over. Mournful cries from the surrounding bush told her the birds were waking. There was no other sound, not that she could detect over the chatter of her teeth.

If he was still out there, she feared he'd hear, so she made an effort to clench her jaw. Taking care not to make any sound, she managed to sit up. It had been too dark during the night to examine her injury. The pain told her it would not be a pretty sight.

Her fingers were blue, swollen and curled over. She didn't bother trying to move them. Harper swallowed and rolled back her sleeve. A coarse breath hissed out from between her gritted teeth. The arm, puffy and unnaturally shiny, resembled an over-ripe plum in colour. Midway between her wrist and elbow, the flesh was torn where a jagged fragment of bone protruded.

Tears welled up in her eyes and mercifully obscured the injury. If she didn't get help soon, she had no doubt, she'd die from shock and exposure. Her only option, risk leaving the security of her hiding place and try to find help. Harper swiped at her tears with her uninjured left arm. She had to calm her thoughts and act.

She tried to think through her next course of action. When he'd chased her, she ran blindly not knowing or caring where she ended up. Now Harper had no idea where she was. *The sun rises in the east*, her mind raced. *That means, if I keep the sun at my back when I'm moving, I'll hit the coast.* It wasn't much of a plan, but it would have to do. If she could reach the coast, that should run her into the trail and maybe other hikers.

She shuffled forward on her butt and hesitated. *Judith.* There were people out there in danger, people she loved. Had he gone after them? Her instincts told her to find help, but could she leave them? *In this condition, I'm no good to anyone.* Maybe, if she could find her way out of this godforsaken place, she could bring back help.

Harper edged her way between the blackened trunks and into the light. Her whole body trembled as a combination of fear and cold struck her. The crackle of leaves and twigs underfoot seemed unnaturally loud.

Staggering to her feet, she paused only long enough to glance up searching for the sun. Still low in the sky, the golden ball hung like a dazzling smudge blanketed by cloud. Satisfied she'd pin-pointed west, Harper cradled her injured right arm with her left and got moving. She exited the safety of her hiding place and headed in what she hoped was the right direction.

Chapter Thirteen

Judith kept her arm around Milly's waist. Their combined breathing filled Milly's ears, blocking out all other sound. Every inch of the dense bush looked the same as the last except for the odd burnt-out tree trunk or dome-shaped termite mound. Milly guessed they'd been moving away from the cliff site for at least fifteen minutes, but it could have been longer.

"I have to stop," she managed to say around pants of breath. "I'm sorry, Jude, but I just need to sit for a second."

Judith's grip loosened. "Okay, but not for long."

Milly's legs folded under her and she sank to the ground. The pain in her skull had receded to a dull thud leaving a high-pitched buzzing that reminded her of the noise the TV made when it malfunctioned. She pressed her right hand to her ear and tried to block out the sound.

"How do you think Harper's pack got in that tree?" Judith crouched down next to her.

Milly could hear the fear in her sister's voice. "What's really going on here?" Milly asked, ignoring Judith's question.

Judith's expression confirmed her suspicions; she knew more than she was letting on. Milly watched her sister's face change from surprised to guarded. The transformation was complete in the blink of an eye, as if a veil dropped over her features, covering her reaction.

"What do you mean?"

Milly sighed. "I might have hit my head and not talked to you in ten years, but I still know when you're hiding something."

Judith looked over Milly's head as if studying something in the forest. "There is something I need to tell you." She turned her attention back to her sister. "And I will. But not now. We have to keep moving and get out of here."

Milly shook her head, sending a cord of agony through her skull. Letting a breath out through her nose, she kept her expression even. She had no intention of moving until she had more information. "So you *do* know what's going on?"

"No. I swear." Judith held her sister's gaze. "You said you can still tell when I'm holding something back, so you should be able to see I'm telling the truth."

Milly regarded her sister. Her blue eyes were red rimmed and puffy. The guarded expression erased to be replaced, by what? Milly wasn't sure. If she had to guess, she'd say Judith was telling the truth, but would she stake her life on it?

"I'm not moving till you tell me what's going on."

Judith screwed up her eyes and shook her head. "That's what I'm trying to tell you." She waved her hand in a dismissive gesture towards the surrounding trees. "I have no idea what's happening. The screaming, Harper's pack, I'm as confused as you are." Judith dropped onto her knees and her shoulders sagged. "There's things I need to tell you, but not about all this and not now." Her tone softened. "We're in danger. I can feel it and so can you. That's all I know."

Milly wanted to believe her. The alternative – that her sister was somehow involved in hurting and terrifying her – seemed too awful to contemplate.

"Here," Judith slipped off the pack and pulled out the water bottle. "Have a sip. There's not much left in this one." She waggled the bottle sending the contents sloshing from side to side. "You've got another full one in the pack, but we need to make it last."

Milly took the bottle and resisted the urge to gulp down the contents. Her throat felt swollen and hot. She took a small sip and handed it back; she noticed her hand, caked in grime and blood, and trembled. Judith had been right; she *could* feel danger. It was almost palpable, like something in the air making her skin tingle and her limbs feel jittery. As if the forest itself were a living being and could hear her thoughts, a rustle too loud to be caused by the wind came from behind them.

The women locked eyes. Judith swung the pack onto her shoulders and grabbed Milly under her arm. "Let's go," she whispered, and the two moved forward.

Milly knew her watch was lost, but she still had her phone in the pack. Even without a signal, it would still show the time. She wanted to ask Judith to stop and check, but the look of grim determination made it clear that her sister had no intention of stopping or slowing down. If she had to guess, judging by the angle of the sun, she'd put the time at around 11:00 a.m. That meant they'd been walking for hours. Maybe three.

The whining in her ears continued, at first disconcerting and annoying, now almost crippling in its persistence. Mercifully, the pain in her skull had retreated to a mild pounding. Around them the forest was an endless wash of trees and bushes with nothing to mark their progress. Apart from the tweeting of birds and the buzz of midges, they'd heard nothing.

"Do you know where we're going?" Milly asked, scratching at her neck where a cluster of insect bites rasped against her collar.

Judith had released her grip on Milly's waist and now walked a few steps ahead of her.

"I'm not sure." Judith stopped and put her hands on her hips. "Based on what Lucas said, we should be almost at a point where we can turn west and expect to start seeing the landscape grow rocky and steep." She let out a deep breath. "To be honest, when we saw Harper's pack and started moving, I didn't stop to consider which way we were headed so now I'm still trying to figure it out."

"So we could be heading away from the hiking trail?" Milly tried to keep the frustration out of her voice. None of this was Judith's fault. Was it?

"I don't think so," she spoke slowly. Milly thought she sounded unsure.

"I haven't heard anyone following us." Milly looked around. "We might be safe to stop for a while."

"If you need a rest, we'll stop." Judith dropped the pack and sat. The carpet of leaves and forest debris crunched under her.

Milly wrapped her arms around her body and lowered herself to the ground. For the time being, exhaustion took precedence over fear. The muscles in her thighs ached. Not with the same intensity as the pain in her back, but she needed rest. Judith looked fatigued. Milly could see it in the stoop of her shoulders and the paleness of her face.

"Can you check the time on my phone?" Suddenly she wanted the comfort of her phone more than anything. Even without a signal, it was a link to the outside world. She could keep track of their progress. It wasn't much, just *something* to hold on to.

"There's no phone in your pack." Judith pulled out an energy bar. "Here, you look done in. This'll help."

Milly was having trouble processing her sister's words. She knew her phone was in her pack. Why would Judith lie?

"I know it's in there. I put it in the pouch on the opposite side to my water bottle." Milly ignored the energy bar in her sister's outstretched hand. "Why are you saying it's not there?" She could hear her voice rising to an accusing pitch, but didn't care.

Judith tossed the bar back in the pack. "It's not there, Mil. If you don't believe me, look for yourself." She pushed the pack towards her sister.

Milly snatched up the blue backpack and plonked it between her legs. Searching it was difficult with one hand. She checked the side pouches; both were empty. The zip compartment on the outside contained a strip of Band-Aids, a couple of packets of tissues and two Ziploc bags. A weight formed in her chest, like something round and hard. She glanced up at Judith. Her expression remained impassive.

Milly flipped the top of the pack open and rummaged through the contents. How could her phone have disappeared? Judith had been the only other person to handle the pack. The weight in her chest dropped and a sickening feeling swept over her. With the nausea came anger. This whole thing had been Judith's idea. She'd got her out here in the middle of nowhere to do what? Punish her? Torture her?

"Why are you doing this?" Milly's voice came out as a tight croak.

"I'm not doing anything," Judith snapped back. "I told you, I don't know what's going on."

"Yeah. Well if that's true, why'd you take my phone?" Milly didn't wait for her to answer. Using her good hand, she pushed off the ground. "Where is it?" She took a step towards Judith and stood over her. "Give me my phone."

Judith scrabbled to her feet. They were standing only centimetres apart. Milly could hear her sister's heavy breathing, there was a glassy look in her eyes.

"Mil, please stop. You need to calm down. You're not thinking clearly." She tried to put her hand on Milly's shoulder, but she shrugged it off.

"I charged my phone in the car and then put it in my pack before we left." Milly pointed at the pack. "You're the only other person to touch…" Her voice trailed off. She put her hand to her neck. She recalled Harper's voice near her ear and her breath on her neck. Harper tugging on the pack from behind. Could she have taken the phone?

Confused, Milly closed her eyes. *If this buzzing would stop, I could think straight.*

"What?" Judith cut through the noise.

Milly opened her eyes and blinked. She hadn't realised she'd spoken her thoughts. Judith's face appeared to fill the world. Milly wanted to go home, wherever that might be. In that moment, anywhere with walls and a bed would do. The trees seemed to crowd in around them and Judith was too close. Milly could feel a knot twisting in her stomach and her chest heaving.

"Did you hear that?" Judith wrapped her hand around Milly's wrist and squeezed.

"Is this some sort of game?" Milly managed around shallow breaths.

"It's not a game." Judith's voice dropped, "If you don't believe anything else, believe me when I say, this is real." She let go of Milly's wrist, pulled the knife out of her front pocket and snapped it open. "There's a rock there." Judith pointed at the ground. "Pick it up and get ready."

A crack, the sound of a thin branch snapping, echoed off the trees. Milly hesitated. There could be no mistaking what she heard. Something large moved beyond her field of vision. Still hyperventilating, she crouched and picked up the rock. Its weight felt good in her hand.

Judith's shoulders were hunched and her body bent forward. She looked like a wrestler getting ready to pounce on her opponent. *This can't be happening*, Milly told herself. *We're near Yallingup for God's sake, the only large dangerous animals in this part of Western Australia are the human kind.*

"We'll stand back-to-back," Judith whispered keeping her eyes focused on the trees. "Whichever way he comes, we'll be ready."

They were in a small clearing, ringed by trees and dense bush. The morning mist had cleared revealing thick scrub varying in colour from lush green to washed-out silvery grey. The vegetation crowed in, making it almost impossible to see beyond the first few metres of green.

"You think it's a man?" A ridiculous question. What else could it be? But isolated and terrified, all sorts of possibilities ran through her mind.

"Yeah," Judith answered. "And we're going to give him one hell of a fight."

In the midst of panic and fear, Milly had time to marvel at the woman her baby sister had become. She was afraid, Milly could see it in the way the knife trembled in her hand. She could hear it in the catch in her sister's voice, yet she stood ready to take on whatever came at them. An old familiar feeling swept over her, she recognised it as a deep protective instinct. Time seemed to evaporate and Judith was eight years old again; small and trusting. Milly, the older sister, wanted to keep her out of harm's way.

"Run," Milly whispered. Cold trickles of sweat formed under her arms and between her breasts.

"What?" Judith's focus shifted to her sister.

"You're fast. You can out run him." Milly nudged her, trying to make her move. "Don't wait for me, just go."

Another crack, this time closer and to the left. A flock of cockatoos took flight, their startled cries mingled with furious flapping to create a deafening chorus.

Judith gasped but stood her ground. "I'm not leaving you. We'll get through this together."

Milly opened her mouth to argue, but the words lodged in her throat. As the birds' cries receded overhead, the unmistakable sound of boots crunching on the forest debris took its place. The footfalls were heavy, lumbering. Cracking and snapping followed as the unseen intruder broke through the trees and rushed the women.

Chapter Fourteen

Harper's tongue felt large and dry inside her mouth, like a strip of Velcro. She'd had nothing to drink since yesterday afternoon. In addition to her injured arm, her whole body felt fragile and achy, almost feverish. She focused on putting one foot in front of the other and moving forward. Each step jarred, sending shockwaves from her feet to her arm.

She turned and, for probably the tenth time, checked the angle of the sun. It was still low in the sky, behind and to her left. She guessed it was around 11 a.m. When she started walking, she promised herself a break every ten minutes, but as the morning dragged on she seemed to be moving at a snail's pace. In addition to her weakened body, the feeling that someone was lurking nearby, ready to pounce, tortured her mind. She began to consider finding another hiding place and crawling inside.

The landscape veered upwards and changed from thick forest to scraggy bush. She spotted a fallen gum, its trunk as thick as a beer barrel. There were scorch marks along one side and near the centre, a gaping hole. Harper leaned her butt against the trunk. She considered pulling her sleeve back and taking another look at her broken arm.

The image of the shiny white fragment jutting out of her skin flashed in her mind and her stomach clenched. No, she couldn't risk setting off a vomiting fit, she was dehydrated enough. She closed her eyes and waited for her stomach to stop cramping.

Something skittered past her ankle making her gasp and stumble forward. She scanned the base of the fallen tree for signs of a snake and spotted a large goanna diving for cover under the blackened bark.

Harper let out a long breath and watched the creature desperately trying to hide itself under the gum tree. Stubby legs moving in slow sweeping jerks and its thick body swaying left and right in an awkward rhythm. A kookaburra let out a peel of laughter. Harper turned her head and spotted the bird on a low-lying branch a few metres away. It turned its head to the side and surveyed the scene. *Probably trying to decide if the goanna's too heavy to pick up and carry*, Harper thought with a shudder. The bird's predatory gaze made her want to pick up a rock and throw it at the creature. She even went as far as looking around for something suitable to hurl before a rustling from the nearby trees reminded her she was as vulnerable as the lizard.

She needed to keep moving. If he was still looking for her, there was no way of knowing how close he might be. She gave the fallen trunk a last, longing look. She considered crawling inside the fallen log. It would be dark and safe, a chance to sleep. *No. If I crawl in, I'll die in there,* she warned herself. *Yes, but at least in there it'll be quiet and peaceful, if he finds me* – she stopped herself. She couldn't allow her mind to dwell on what might happen. There were people depending on her, one of them Judith. Her feelings for Judith were almost frightening in their intensity. The thought of him hurting her, or worse, was more than Harper could stand.

She moved away from the goanna and the rapacious kookaburra, and continued forward. She tried to figure out how many more hours it would take her to reach the coast. At her current pace, it couldn't be more than one or two. *If I'm going in the right direction.* She looked over her shoulder; the sun high in the sky was partially draped in wispy grey clouds. Had it been lower when she last checked? She couldn't remember how long she'd spent resting. It had seemed like only minutes, but could her mind be playing tricks on her?

Behind her came the sound of footfalls on lose ground. Harper let out a wail and clutched her injured arm to her body. He'd found her. She picked up her pace, and did her best to run. She'd wasted so much time when she should have been running, trying to find help.

Turning her head from left to right, she searched for a hiding place. *Maybe he hasn't seen me and I can wait him out again*, her desperate mind tried to latch on to the frail hope before a flat voice in her mind piped up – *if you can hear him, he can hear you.*

Her only hope was silence. She stopped moving forward and side-stepped. Crouching in a cluster of spindly bushes, no more than a metre or so high, she waited and listened. *I'll hear him, but he won't hear me.* Her hair had come lose and hung around her face in stringy clumps. She counted silently. When she reached forty, the sound of boots, distant but distinct, became audible. All sound ceased. Harper closed her eyes and screwed up her face as if waiting for a blow to land. She counted.

Fifteen seconds then the sound of someone large and heavy changing direction, pivoting and then moving. She'd read somewhere, maybe in a thriller, that sound carries farther in the wilderness because of the absence of other sound. If that were true, maybe he was farther away than he seemed. *Or maybe he's like the devil and can move without sound.* She knew the thought was nothing more than childish fear trying to overtake her, but just the same it sent an icy finger running down her spine.

The idea of standing and looking around took her breath away. She imagined him waiting only metres away, a vacuous smile lighting up his brutal face. Harper kept her eyes tightly shut and continued to count. If she reached three hundred and sixty, ten minutes without hearing him, she'd stand. Besides, there was something comforting and lulling in counting. The mind-numbing familiarity of numbers soothed the pain and gave her something to cling to.

Chapter Fifteen

Judith moved first. Raising the knife to shoulder height, she stepped forward and let out a howl. The figure collapsed at her feet sending a spray of grit and seedpods flying.

"No!" Everything happened so quickly, Milly couldn't be sure of what she'd seen. Or, if Judith had used the knife. "Don't, Jude. It's Lucas." Milly dropped the rock and grabbed her sister's arm.

For a moment, the two women stood over him, both unsure what to do next. Lucas groaned and rolled onto his back. His face streaked with blood and his shirt torn, he blinked but seemed unaware of his surroundings.

"He's hurt," Milly crouched down near his head. "Did you stab him?" She asked, looking up at her sister.

"No. I didn't touch him." Judith made no move to help Milly with the injured man. "He just collapsed in front of me."

"Put the knife away and get him some water." Milly wondered why her sister just stood there. She could feel the adrenalin still coursing through her body. She guessed Judith was feeling the same way. "Quick, he needs help."

Judith nodded and dropped the pack. Milly turned her attention back to the injured man. "Lucas?" Milly waited a few seconds. His eyes were open, but seemed unfocused. "Lucas, look at me," she tried using a sharper tone.

It seemed to work. He blinked a few times then his dark eyes shifted and locked on hers. Milly noticed a gash on his forehead surrounded by swelling. The right sleeve of his shirt was torn and hanging down around his elbow, revealing a shiny muscular bicep. His clothes were filthy as if he'd been crawling through the dirt. He reminded Milly of footage she'd seen on the news; survivors running from a building that'd just been bombed. He had the same haunted look on his face as those terrified people.

"Lucas?" she tried again. "What happened to you?"

His mouth moved and he managed to croak out a few sounds.

"Where's Harper?" Judith asked. She crouched on the other side of him holding the water bottle.

"Give him a drink." Milly felt irritated by her sister's lack of action, but tried to keep it out of her voice. If her back wasn't injured, Milly would have reached over and snatched the bottle from her and given Lucas a drink by now.

Judith held the bottle to Lucas's mouth. He managed to raise himself onto his elbows and open his mouth. Milly watched his throat work as he sucked down the water. Something played around the edges of her mind, just out of reach. She tried to bring the thought to the foreground of her thinking, but it slipped away from her.

"Not too much at once," Milly reached out her hand and gently pulled the bottle from his lips.

Lucas let out a deep sigh and lay back. The circle of trees cast a gloomy shadow over his face. He closed his eyes and within seconds his chest rose and fell like someone in a deep sleep. Milly tried calling his name a few times but he remained unresponsive. Finally, she gave up and sank onto her hip besides him.

"You're not supposed to let people with head injuries sleep," she said, looking over at Judith who sat on his other side. "Do you think he's asleep or unconscious?"

"We need to find Harper." She pointed at Lucas. "Something's happened to them. They never made it out of here, so that means Harper is still nearby. I think we should start searching for her."

Milly nodded. It made sense, but what about Lucas. Harper was her friend, but she couldn't just abandon the man.

"Yeah. You're right, but let's give him a few minutes."

The two women moved a couple of metres away and sat together watching the unconscious man. Milly could see his chest rise and fall and hear his breathing, deep and steady. She looked up, the sun sat high in the milky blue sky. She guessed it must be around midday.

"Jude," she turned to her sister. She noticed Judith's legs were smeared with dirt, knees grubby from kneeling on the ground. She supposed she looked even worse. Milly raked her dirty fingers through her short dark hair. "You said you had things to tell me; I think now's the time."

Judith nodded. She took the lighter out of the top pocket of her shirt and flicked it on. She watched the flame for a few seconds. It was a cheap plastic job, orange with a black top. Milly hadn't thought of it before, but she began to wonder why her sister carried a lighter when she didn't smoke. Maybe it was a camping thing she didn't know about. She thought of asking her but dismissed the idea. Judith obviously had something she needed to get off her chest, muddying the waters with pointless questions wouldn't help.

"Harper and I," Judith blew the flame out and curled her fist over the lighter. "We're close."

"I know. She told me you two still keep in touch, but what does…"

"No." Judith shook her head. Her bouncy brown hair looked lank and clung to the sides of her face. "I mean we're *really* close."

Milly opened her mouth to speak and then the meaning of her sister's words sunk in. Her mind reeled. What Judith was saying didn't make sense, Harper loved men. In high school she always had boyfriends. And Judith, how could Milly not know?

"Are you saying that you and Harper…" She let her words hang in the air, not sure how to finish the question.

Judith nodded and put the lighter back in her pocket. "We moved in together about six months ago. But…" She shrugged. "We've been together for about two years."

"Did Mum know?"

"Yes. She knew. It's not something I've ever tried to hide. I've been open about myself for years." She turned and looked at her sister. Judith's cheeks were flushed and her eyes filled with tears. "I'm sorry we didn't tell you before, but Harper said you were too fragile and she didn't want to upset you."

The shock of Judith's revelation started to fade, replaced by a grim flicker of anger. Everyone had known but her. Even her mother. Her mind raced over all the phone conversations, never once had her mum mentioned anything about Judith and Harper. It was as if Milly were a stranger to her own family. Milly sucked in her bottom lip. Harper was supposed to be her friend, yet she'd kept her in the dark all this time.

"What else have you lied about?" The throbbing in Milly's head made her wince and narrow her eyes. She wanted to get up and run away. Put as much distance between herself and her sister as possible. Instead, she waited for Judith to answer.

"This trip." Judith swallowed. "Harper and I planned it together."

"Yeah, that seems pretty obvious *now*." Milly couldn't keep the anger out of her voice. "The only thing I don't get is why. Or is that obvious too?"

"What?" Judith frowned.

"The money," Milly said in a flat voice. "You wanted me to agree to whatever scheme you and Harper cooked up. Probably talk me into signing my share of Mum's house and all the income from her books over to you." Milly waved her arm towards Lucas. "Is that what all this is about? Frighten me into doing whatever you want?" Her voice wavered as a new and more horrifying thought occurred. "Or were you going to get rid of me?"

Judith shook her head and the tears spilled onto her cheeks. "No," her voice was high with indignation. "We never meant to hurt you."

"So this *is* about the money?" Milly paused. "And you *did* hurt me." She pointed at Lucas. "And him."

Judith put her hand on Milly's leg. Milly curled her lip and jerked herself sideways. "I thought …" She stopped herself. She didn't want to break down. If she let herself cry, she didn't think she'd be able to stop. "I just want to get out of here."

"I know," Judith spoke softly. "But just let me explain."

Milly looked around. The trees seemed to be crowding in, blocking out the light and casting shadows that reminded her of talons. Her stomach clenched, she needed her pills.

"We *did* plan this trip together and," she hesitated. "And *some* of what happened, but it was never about money and no one was supposed to get hurt."

Milly stared at her sister, horrified by her confession. Judith and Harper *had* planned this. Harper, her oldest friend, her ally. The betrayal was almost inconceivable.

"We just wanted to get you out here so you and I could spend some time alone. They were supposed to let you climb down the cliff and drop you a couple of metres from the ground." Judith let out a long shaky breath. "Just scare you, nothing serious." She rubbed her hand across her forehead. "Something went wrong. I don't know what happened. I swear."

"You said 'they.'" Milly felt tears stinging her eyes and tried to blink them away.

"What?" Judith seemed thrown off balance.

"You said, *they* were supposed to let me climb down." Milly looked over at the unconscious man. "He's in on it too?"

Judith opened her mouth to answer and then closed it again. She dropped her chin and stared into her lap. Milly let the silence stretch out between them. In the trees nearby, birds twittered happily.

"Yes. Well, sort of."

"Is he part of this or not?" Milly needed to know and at the same time dreaded the answer. The thought of the three of them planning, conspiring against her – laughing – it made her feel small, stupid, and very alone. *It's safe, I promise. You'll be surprised how easy it is,* the words Judith and Lucas had used to coax her into stepping over the edge of the cliff pinged around in her mind.

"We barely know him. Harper met him at the gym and he … I don't know how he got so involved. Judith ran her fingers through her hair. He gave us some abseiling lessons in the bush around Kalamunda. I told him about wanting to spend a few days with you." She shook her head. Lucas suggested we come out here. He liked the idea of bringing the two of us together using tough love." Judith shrugged. "He went along with it."

"Did you pay him?" Milly barely recognised her own voice; it sounded older, tired. Like the voice of an elderly woman that's been beaten down by life's disappointments.

Judith nodded. Milly looked away from her sister at the man lying at the edge of the trees. She could see his chest moving, he was still breathing. He meant nothing to her, she only met him yesterday and even then hadn't really liked him. She wondered why his betrayal should hurt so much.

"It sounds pathetic now but I had my reasons and they're not all selfish."

Milly laughed, an unpleasant sound lacking any joy or humour. "Let me guess, you did this for me. To help me?" She thumped her hand against her chest. "You paid someone to drop me over a cliff and nearly kill me, for what? My own good?" Milly stretched her mouth into a humourless grin. The cut on her lip pulled open and she felt blood ooze down her chin.

"I needed to know the truth. I thought if we were out here, just the two of us, and you were afraid, you'd tell me." Judith looked into her sister's eyes. "I can't go on until I know what really happened … It has haunted me. The blame, the guilt." Her voice dropped to a whisper. "That night … at the Reach, it's tainted every day since. Tell me what happened."

Milly reeled back as if she'd been slapped. She'd dreaded this moment. The nerves, the anxiety about seeing Judith again. She'd known deep down it would always come back to this. Judith would never stop hounding her.

"I've told you a million times. You got Drew killed with your stupid attention seeking." Her voice rose to nearly a scream.

Judith drew back. "I know you were back in Angel Fern."

Milly couldn't believe what she was hearing. How could Judith know about the hospital? The buzzing in her ears intensified. After all these years, she'd allowed herself to believe there might be a chance at re-establishing a bond with her sister, but it had all been lies and manipulation.

"I saw the bills when I went through Mum's things. I know you've been hospitalised three times in the last ten years." Judith shook her head. "This has to stop, Mil.

That's why Harper and I brought you out here." She reached out to her sister. "For you and for me."

Milly struggled to her feet. "So all that screaming last night, if that was to scare me, you and Harper can pat each other on the back because it worked. I…"

"No. I don't know what that was. Everything else I said, about being in danger," Judith stood and looked around. "I meant it. I might have brought you out here, but something else is happening. We need to find Harper and get out of here."

They were in agreement on one thing, Milly wanted to leave as quickly as possible. She had no interest in anything else her sister had to say, including the whole *we're in danger* routine. She turned away and moved to where Lucas lay.

Milly crouched over him. In repose, his face looked calm, almost perfect. So different from the gruff monosyllabic bore he'd turned out to be. Whatever he'd done. Taken money from her sister to do … what? Trick her? Help terrorise her? As much as it hurt, she couldn't turn her back on an injured man.

"Lucas?" she snapped the word and patted his cheek.

His eyes flickered open then held hers. He raised his hand to the side of his forehead and groaned. Judith must have heard him stir. Her boots pounded across the small clearing.

"What happened?" Judith knelt beside him and leaned in. "Where's Harper?"

Lucas pulled himself into a sitting position with his knees drawn up. "I don't know." He dragged the back of his hand across his forehead smearing blood on his arm. "Things happened so fast. One minute we were heading back towards the trail." He paused and looked from Judith to Milly. "Then everything went crazy."

Chapter Sixteen

Harper pushed herself into a crouching position and raised her head until she could see over the top of the bushes. It had been nearly twenty-four hours since she'd last had water, or food. She knew she could go without eating for days and still survive, but without water, she couldn't last much longer. Her muscles were cramping and bouts of dizziness became more frequent. Sustaining the awkward stance for more than a few seconds took every ounce of willpower she had left.

It had been at least ten minutes since she'd last heard his footfalls. She scanned the bushes and trees for any sign of movement. If he was nearby, she couldn't hear him. Every tree or cluster of vegetation looked like a possible hiding place. She couldn't dismiss the possibility that he might be waiting her out. If she broke from the relative safety of the bushes, he might pounce. Harper grasped the hem of her shirt and squeezed it in her fist. *Move or hide*, the question repeated over and over in her mind.

The distant cry of seagulls caught her attention. She turned her head in what had to be a westerly direction. *I must be close*. Her heart beat kicked up a couple of notches. The trail leading back to the carpark had to be within a twenty-minute walk. If she could make it that far, there was a strong chance she might meet other hikers.

Harper stretched her legs and stood. She waited a beat and then turned west. The sun, now high in the sky, was on her right. Grey autumn clouds filtered much of its warmth, but the weak rays on her back were enough to raise a slick of sweat under the hair on the back of her neck. Her boots felt heavy on the end of her legs, lifting them took effort. With each step the bush thinned until she recognised the barren coastal plains from the day before. A warm feeling blossomed in her chest – hope.

She pictured the parking lot, the toilet block, square and bland with luke-warm water on tap. She licked her cracked lips and forced her legs to keep moving. Soon it would be over. She'd find help; *there's safety in numbers*. Maybe a group of hikers. Harper's mind seized onto the idea. They'd have phones. How long would it take the police to arrive? Judith and Milly couldn't be far away. If they brought in rescue helicopters they'd be able to spot them almost immediately. Her mind tried to throw up *what ifs*, but Harper resisted the grim images that wanted to form in her head.

Her boots struck rock. "Nearly there," the sound of her voice was little more than a dry croak.

The stony ground set her off balance. She slowed her pace. If she fell and landed on her broken arm, she wouldn't be able to get back up. The thought of coming so far only to lie dying among the barren rocks brought tears to her eyes. A blast of wind blew her hair back and filled her nose with the tang of salty air. She picked her way forward, face tilted up to the breeze.

Something shifted in the distance. Her heart thudded, sending a tremor through her chest. She stopped moving, eyes trained on the movement. Could he have circled around and got ahead of her? It was possible, she'd been so focused on keeping her balance. He could have passed her at a distance. There were still snatches of vegetation, he could have been ghosting her the whole time.

Chapter Seventeen

He moved from tree to tree, stepping around twigs and fallen branches. Sweat ran down his forehead and neck in warm streams. He paused and sniffed the air, imagining himself as a wolf hunting its prey. He'd heard her before. Of that he was certain. There could be no mistaking her terrified footfalls darting through the bush. He was close.

He licked his lips. His mouth felt sandy. Blondie's fault. When she managed to wriggle out of his grasp, he'd left everything and took off after her. Now he couldn't risk going back for water, not when he was so close to finding her. *When I get hold of her, I'll take her back with me. I'll enjoy her more after I've had a drink.* He rubbed his forearm against his mouth. *Yeah*, he liked that plan.

It didn't take a genius to guess where she was heading; back to the trail. *Looking for help*, an obvious move. But clever little Blondie had somehow managed to head in the right direction, that's what surprised him most. He tapped his fingers against his thigh. She was starting to irritate him. He could feel the blood whooshing around in his veins. Blondie was supposed to be an easy mark. An added bonus to the main event, but thanks to her ducking and diving, he could think of nothing else.

He felt a surge of helplessness. If she reached the trail, he *could* lose her. Everything he'd planned and dreamed of would go up in smoke. *No*, he told himself. *I'm the one running this circus. No one fucks with me and gets away with it.* His mind threw up an image of Allan – meaty hands, like ham hocks stroking his face. He pushed the memory away. And focused on how Allan looked years later when his foster son returned.

* * *

"It's good to see you, kid." He stood in the doorway of the shit tip he called a house. There was fear in the restless shifting of his eyes. It felt good to see him that way. He'd seemed so big all those years ago, but time and heavy drinking had shrivelled him into a trembling old man.

He pushed past Allan and walked into the house. The stink of cigarettes and piss nearly made him gag. "So you came back to visit old Allan, did you?" He gave a nervous laugh that turned into a phlegmy cough.

He watched Allan shuffle over to his chair. Grunting with the effort, he lowered himself. His watery eyes darted around the room as if looking for something.

"You look like shit." He spoke for the first time. The old man winced then tried to laugh it off.

"I've been sick." He patted his chest with yellowed fingers. "It's my lungs. Doctor says I should give up the smokes." He reached out to the side table next to his chair where a blue clay ashtray overflowed with butts. He pulled a cigarette out of a battered pack and shoved it between his lips. "Old habits." He sniffed and lit the smoke. His fingers shook.

"Problems with your lungs?" He made his voice soft and concerned.

"Yeah. Yeah." Allan regarded him through a cloud of smoke. He looked relieved. "I'm not in a good way. But it's good you came to see me." He coughed and then pulled a filthy rag out of his jeans. He spat something into the square of fabric and stuffed it back in his pocket. "But I'm supposed to have a visit from the health nurse." He made a big show of looking at the clock over the fireplace. "She'll be here soon."

He nodded as if believing Allan's story. "If you're expecting a visitor, we'll have to be quick." He watched the old man, letting his words sink in.

Allan's eyes, small and buried in folds of grey skin widened. "What… what do you mean, kid?"

He reached behind him and pulled the knife out from its sheaf. For a moment he just held it, giving the old man time to get a really good look at the size of the blade.

Allan started to stand. "Look, if this is about all that stuff when you were a kid." He shook his head. "You know I was drinking a lot." He dropped the cigarette. It bounced on the threadbare carpet. "I'm sorry, kid. Don't do anything crazy." His voice was high, almost a squeal.

"You got problems with your lungs?" He smiled and crossed the room. "Let's get them out and take a look."

Allan fell back into the chair as if all the strength had been sucked out of him. His mouth opened and a wheezy croak burst through his few remaining teeth. Before the old man had time to suck up enough breath to protest, he was on him.

* * *

He blinked.

He hadn't realised he'd stopped moving. How much time had he lost? Around him, birds chattered. He looked up. A pair of multi-coloured rosellas watched him with dumb curiosity. As much as he enjoyed reliving his last moments with Allan, he had more pressing business. As if by magic, he spotted movement between the trees.

He got a blurred glimpse of something pale darting behind a copse of trees. "There you are." He pulled the knife out from its home against the small of his back. She couldn't be more than five minutes ahead of him. His heart rate quickened and he felt a tingle run up between his groin and navel.

Chapter Eighteen

Harper turned and checked behind her. Spindly grey native shrubs shuddered in the breeze. No sign of movement. She turned her attention back to the shifting figure in the distance. In the seconds since she'd turned away, it had progressed south. She took a couple of steps and squinted trying to make out any details.

The shape coalesced into a clear human form. Harper took another step, quick like a square dancer. Her eyes picked out some detail. The figure appeared tall, but that could have been an optical illusion created by the angle and the distance. He held something in his hand. *A knife.* She quickly dismissed the idea, the object appeared long and thin, reaching from the man's hand to the ground. *A walking stick.*

"Please, please, please," she muttered willing the figure to be anyone but *him.*

Harper stumbled forward trying to keep her eyes on the person and maintain her balance at the same time. Now, less than thirty metres away, she could see his outline clearly. Thin, slightly stooped, using a long walking stick – definitely male. He was moving at a steady pace.

From this distance and in her weakened condition, she'd never catch him.

She snatched another look behind. Nothing but scrub and stone. When she turned back, he'd progressed farther south. His outline began to blur. Harper fought back panic. If she tried to run, she risked falling. The man would disappear from view without ever seeing her. Her only option was to call for help and risk attracting the wrong attention.

With time running out, Harper let out a wail. "Help!" A plea that sounded more like a weak groan.

The figure continued moving. Harper licked her lips and took and deep shuddering breath, "Help!" This time louder. "Help, please!" She raised her uninjured arm and waved it above her head.

Across the expanse, the figure stopped walking. Something fluttered near his head. His form turned, the stick poised over the ground as if frozen in motion. Harper took another step and waved her arm, this time in a wide arc from her side then up and over her head.

"Help," she stretched the word out into one long call, until all the breath left her lungs.

The figure seemed to be standing still but somehow growing bigger and clearer until Harper realised he was jogging towards her. The walking stick became a long, blue, narrow walking pole. The fluttering around his head, a red legionnaire's hat. The figure turned into a tall elderly man dressed rather comically with long bony legs visible below overly baggy shorts.

Harper's cracked lips drew back into a pained smile. She staggered to a large pink slab of rock and sat down. *I made it*. If she wasn't so exhausted, she'd have laughed with relief. Her head drooped forward until it nearly touched her knees. She'd come so far, but the thought of standing up to greet the stranger seemed harder than the hours of walking.

"Hey? Are you hurt?" His voice rang clear and high with concern and curiosity.

In front of her, Harper saw two scuffed, mustard coloured boots topped with red socks. She looked up. Her first impression had been correct, her saviour was an elderly man – mid-sixties, maybe older and shaped like an overgrown stick insect.

He crouched in front of her. Harper raised her head, chin wobbling. His eyes were green, buried in a nest of wrinkles. Up close, his skin looked thin, like greyish parchment. She could smell Palmolive soap and something sweet, maybe humbugs.

"Are you hurt?" The surprise had left his voice, he sounded calm.

Harper nodded and touched her injured arm.

"Alright. I'm going to move your sleeve so I can have a look. I'll be very gentle and I promise, I won't hurt you." He had a slight accent, English. She heard kindness in his tone and a level of reassurance that brought tears to her eyes. If she could have stood, she'd have fallen into his arms sobbing. Instead, she hiccupped out a sob and bobbed her head.

"My name's William by the way. William Walterson." He waited a beat for her to respond.

"H… Harper."

"Alright then, Harper." He touched the edge of the fabric and raised it above her skin.

Harper's stomach clenched and she clamped her teeth together in anticipation of what she was about to see. William swept the sleeve towards her upper arm slowly and with an unexpected deftness. If he was shocked by what he saw, he showed no sign. Harper caught a glimpse of the wound. Purple flesh, puffy and streaked with red surrounding a lump of what looked like blackcurrant jam. A shaft of white protruding from the sticky mess.

William moved his head so his red legionnaire's hat blocked her view of the injury. "This is quite nasty. A grade two open fracture, I'm afraid. Surgery." He made a clicking sound with his tongue. "Probably two surgeries and a lengthy rehabilitation, but nothing a strong young woman like you can't manage."

Harper nodded. "Are you? I … thank you." She didn't know how to respond. The pain and fear of the last twenty-four hours seemed to descend on her all at once. Her body shook and her teeth began to chatter.

William slipped out of his jacket and draped it around her shoulders. It was a smooth movement, like something a dashing gentleman might do in an old movie. He pulled a water bottle from a small grey pack near his feet. He unscrewed the cap with long graceful fingers and pressed it into her good hand.

She didn't need to be told, Harper drank. The water washed over her parched throat like rain hitting a shrivelled sponge. The sweetness of the cool clean water was beyond anything she'd imagined. William placed a restraining hand on her forearm.

"Slowly," he cautioned. "Small sips or you'll make yourself sick."

Harper forced herself to slow down and breathe between sips. She watched William rifle through his miniature pack. He'd pulled her sleeve back down and covered her wound. The way he'd spoken about her injury, calmly and with medical knowledge made her wonder if he was a doctor.

"Are you a doctor?" She knew she should be telling him what happened to her, warning him. Yet, his presence calmed her and she found herself asking stupid questions.

"Yes. I'm an orthopaedic surgeon." He looked up from his pack. "Retired." He held up a very early model iPhone. "Here it is. My late wife made me promise I'd always carry a phone when hiking." He pulled off his hat revealing a head of wispy white hair. "Now, I'm going to telephone the police and give them our location. I'll need to know if you're part of a group and if so, where your friends might be."

The police. Her friends. The words galvanised her and her story started tumbling out. "I was with a group. There was an accident. My friend fell. She's hurt. My girlfriend's with her. We're all in danger, a…"

William's fingers hovered over the screen. "Danger? What sort of danger?"

Harper shook her head. "Call the police, please. Just call them." She tried to stand, but William put his hand on her shoulder. "Don't try to get up. You're experiencing shock."

She could see the screen, he'd pressed zero. "Call the police," her voice cracked. "He's out there. There's no time."

"Who's out there?" William held the phone, his finger poised over the screen. "Is it one of your friends?"

"Yes. I mean no. It's …" dizziness swamped her and William's green eyes swam in a watery soup. His voice sounded hollow, the words long and exaggerated. He spoke again and Harper felt as if she'd been jerked back to the sound. The cool sea breeze, the sound of birds crying all rushed in with a sudden blast.

"I think your friend's coming now," William said, looking over her head.

"What?" Harper felt like she was a beat behind, trying to keep up with what was happening. She looked up at William and saw his eyes widen then narrow. He fumbled with the phone.

Still sitting, Harper turned from the waist. The movement felt slow and deliberate as if her whole body knew what to expect and shrank from the inevitable. He moved between the salt bushes, striding forward, wide powerful shoulders moving in a swinging motion powered by long thick legs. His body an immense presence made more threatening by the stealth of his approach and the hunting knife held loosely at his side.

"Call the police." Harper turned back to William.

"Yes. I'm doing so, but I'm afraid we might have to handle this ourselves." He pressed the last zero and held the phone an inch or so from his ear. The only sign of fear came from the slight tremor in his hand. "Stand up and move behind me."

"But… He's… You won't…"

"Now. Without argument," William's voice rose slightly; a man used to giving life or death orders.

Harper clambered to her feet with energy she didn't know she had left and scurried behind the elderly doctor. Her injured arm pulsed in time with her heart beat. She could hear the phone ringing near William's ear. He bent with surprising agility and snatched his hiking pole up from the sand.

"Stop there!" William's voice rang out, clear and confident as if he were addressing a lecture theatre full of medical students not a madman brandishing a huge knife. "I've called the police, they're on their way."

His approach faltered. Harper craned her neck around William watching her tormentor. For an instant, she almost believed he might stop, but then a smile drew the corners of his mouth up and he continued towards them. His black pants were dusty and ripped around one knee and his arms were stained with grime as if he'd been crawling through the dirt. He moved with the easy assurance of one who has all the time in the world.

The air smelt tangy and metallic as if charged with electricity. Harper wrapped the fingers of her left hand around a swatch of William's shirt. From the phone came the sound of a recorded voice, female and nasal.

"He'll kill us both," Harper didn't bother to whisper. She pulled on William's shirt trying to draw him backwards even as she realised there was nowhere to go.

As the man with the knife drew nearer, William's voice faltered. "Put the knife down."

William allowed Harper to pull him back a few steps. They shuffled together like awkward dance partners trying to work in reverse. Harper kept her eyes on the knife. The man who'd spent twenty-four hours hunting her raised his thick forearm and brandished the blade, moving it through the air in a wide sweeping motion.

"You shouldn't have dragged the old guy into this." He looked around William and shook his head. "Shame on you hiding behind a coot like him." His voice was full of disapproval and teasing, but his dark eyes were flat and emotionless.

William lifted the hiking pole and let his long elegant fingers slide half way down the shaft. He still held the phone loosely at his side.

"Run." William jerked forward breaking Harper's grasp on his shirt and putting himself closer to the knife.

Harper stumbled sideways, a high-pitched keening burst through her lips. She faltered, torn between the urge to flee and the realisation of what was about to happen. Before she could make another move, the man with the knife stepped in and batted the pole sideways with his left hand.

William grunted and dropped the phone. It hit the sand with a dull thud. He managed to keep hold of the pole even as the younger man pulled it towards him, moving William around like a rag doll. Harper saw the knife slice through the air; the man gripping it bared his teeth, his scarred cheeks creasing with the effort, as he drove the weapon into the side of William's neck. The blade sank into the elderly man's flesh with thick wet *whack*. Arterial blood spurted, bright red and urgent, in a spray powerful enough to paint the surrounding rocks in oily red splatter.

Harper tottered back a few steps, bent forward and screamed, her lungs straining with the force and volume of the cry.

The younger man held onto the knife's handle and let gravity pull it from the wound as William's legs folded, sinking to the ground. The gash continued to spurt in a wide arc soaking the assailant's black pants, pooling around his boots. Before William hit the ground, his right arm shot forward in what looked like a spasm and the tip of the pole sank into the younger man's side.

He let out a petulant howl and raised his boot, kicking William backwards. William let out a hollow breath as his body crumpled. Two more weak spurts escaped from the wound in his neck and pattered the sand like a sprinkling of summer rain. William dropped onto his back, he shuddered once and then lay still.

Harper's screams turned into weak gasps. William lay in a puddle of dark liquid already soaking into the grainy sand. The man with the knife pressed his hand to his side and groaned. Harper felt a momentary flicker of satisfaction. William had wounded him. Now *he* was the one hurting. The feeling was quickly replaced by panic. He was only a few metres away, even if she were uninjured and in the best condition of her life, the chances of outrunning him over uneven rocky ground were almost zero. She felt cornered in the huge expanse of wilderness.

He wiped the blade on his thigh leaving a smear of sticky goo on his black pants; his movements slow and precise. For a moment, he regarded William's body. He tapped the knife against his leg as if deep in thought. Harper shuffled a few paces west. The path William had been walking couldn't be more than thirty metres away. Maybe there'd be more traffic, someone might come by at any moment. A glimmer of hope materialised with a wave of guilt and shame. She'd seen what he'd done to William. As if to reinforce her shame, the rusty smell of blood wafted towards her.

Run. It came like a switch being turned on in her brain. She'd stayed ahead of him this far, maybe she could keep going. As if he'd read her mind, the man looked up and their eyes locked. He couldn't have been more than twenty-five yet he looked worn. His features were thick and the skin on his cheeks mottled by acne scars.

"You've made things harder for me and yourself," he spoke casually as if they'd been in the middle of a conversation before William arrived and not a death race. "No more hide and seek." He stepped over William's body.

Harper turned, her boots scrunching the sand. The jacket William had draped around her shoulders dropped in a heavy heap. She knew he was expecting her to run towards the path so she leaned forward and pumped her arms as if heading towards the coast, then immediately side-stepped and darted left in a southerly direction.

Clutching her injured arm to her stomach slowed her down and threw her off balance, but the water had done wonders. She kept her eyes on the rocks and salt bush roots that criss-crossed the terrain and managed to pick up a bit of steam. Behind her, she heard him swearing and stomping after her. He sounded close, but she didn't dare look back. To look behind her would cost time and focus, something she couldn't risk.

The landscape bumped and bounced ahead as her lungs burned. She'd almost reached the end of her strength, she knew her body couldn't continue to burn so hard. *I won't make it easy for him*, the thought pushed her on. Not the belief that she could out run him again, but the determination to punish him in the only way left to her, making him run. It was all she had left to hold on to.

The costal flora thickened. Salt bushes that in some areas were waist high, grew taller and widely spaced until they arched overhead casting long cage-like shadows. Harper focused on a patch of light ten or fifteen metres away. *I'll make it to the light,* she told herself. *I won't die in the shadows*. Her thighs burned and her heart pulsed in her throat. A few more steps and she'd be out of the trees. *I'll see the sky again.* Her stride faltered as something grabbed her hair.

Her scalp jerked with enough force to lift her eyebrows and send a burning sensation across her face. Her legs still moving, ran out from under her and she felt herself tipping backwards.

"Got you." His voice waved with breathlessness, but he sounded triumphant. "You're like a fucking rabbit." The words came out separated by wet gasps for air.

He hauled her to her feet by the hair. Harper twisted sideways. The searing in her scalp sent shivers down her spine. He wrapped his arm around her waist, crushing her broken arm under his grasp. White light, as if she'd been staring into the sun, filled Harper's vision. The pain in her arm was like barbed wire being dragged under her skin. She felt the fight drain out of her body and she slumped against him.

"Judith." She didn't know if she'd thought it or heard it. Blackness, soft and warm pushed the light away.

"Don't worry, I'll look after your girlfriend." His words spiralled downwards and followed her into unconsciousness.

Chapter Nineteen

"Two guys. I thought they were hikers." Lucas took another sip of water. "We met them on our way back. Harper and I were moving fast; you know, to get help for you." He looked at Milly. He seemed to want to say more, but then went back to the story. "They were headed south. Harper tried her phone, but no signal." He squinted his eyes. "No. I'm getting it mixed up."

Judith slid onto her butt and drew her knees up mirroring Lucas's position. "It's okay. Just tell us what you remember." Her words were encouraging, but Milly could hear the frustration in her sister's voice.

"The two guys. They stopped and asked us if we needed help." He gave a grunt. "I suppose we looked panicked. Harper started telling them about you two and what had happened." He paused. "I didn't like the way they were looking at her. I could see they weren't interested in what she was saying. They kept nodding, but I had a bad feeling ... You can meet some strange people when you're hiking."

"What did they do to Harper?" Judith's voice sounded tight as if she were bracing herself for the worst.

"That's just it, I don't know. I told the guys we had to keep moving and sort of grabbed Harper's arm." He held Milly's gaze. "You were unconscious when we left, I didn't know how badly you were hurt so I didn't want to waste any time. Besides there was something off about the two men. Their clothes were new, like this was their first time … Almost like they were trying too hard to look like hikers." He seemed to be thinking. "I pulled Harper away and sort of talked over my shoulder, you know trying to get away before anything happened."

Milly didn't like where the story was headed. She could see Lucas had taken some blows. He was a big guy; if they'd overpowered him, what chance did Harper stand? She glanced over at her sister, her face had drained of colour lending a greyish tinge to her skin. Milly guessed Judith had to be thinking the same thing.

"So you pulled Harper away. Then what?" Judith prompted.

"They started following us. Harper got angry. She pulled away from me and turned back. She told the two of them to get fucked." He took another sip from the bottle. "Nothing happened for a second. The two guys looked, well, sort of pleased." Lucas made a sound in his throat, a cross between a chuckle and a groan. "I pushed Harper behind me. That's when they jumped me. The older one sort of tackled me. I threw a few punches. I think I landed one, but the younger one slammed me in the side of the head." He put his hand to the wound and winced. "I blacked out. When I woke up, Harper was gone and so was all our stuff. By then it was dark. I wandered around for hours. Then I heard the screaming. I walked most of the night trying to find her." He shook his head and stared down at his hands.

Milly glanced at her sister and didn't like what she saw. Her fine brows were drawn together, her mouth tight. Milly braced herself for a barrage of questions. Instead, Judith nodded. *Maybe I've misread her again*. Milly thought of asking her sister if she was okay, but Lucas resumed his story and the moment passed. "I got turned around. I only stopped and sat down to get my bearings ... I must have passed out again." He looked back up and his eyes shifted between the two women. "Then I found you two."

Milly put her hand over Lucas's. He wrapped his fingers around hers. His dark eyes looked almost black against the whites. She'd been so angry with him, with Judith and Harper, but the anguish in his voice struck at something deep inside her. The part of her that knew what it was to make a mistake. To fail someone and need forgiveness. If she held on to the anger, she'd be a hypocrite. Any doubts she had about her sister being genuinely scared were gone.

"We need to get back to the trail." Milly nodded to Judith. "Lucas needs a doctor." She touched the back of her head. "So do I." She looked up, the sky was visible in snatches. Judging by the crispness of the light, she guessed it had to be around midday. She glanced at Lucas's wrist and saw a white strip of skin, but no watch.

"We can't just go." Judith stood over them. "Harper's still out here somewhere, we need to find her." She bent and took the water bottle from Lucas's hand. "And we don't have much water left."

"Judith!" Milly didn't know what to say. Her sister's aggression seemed misplaced and out of character. *I guess I barely know her.* Milly thought of Judith's plan to isolate and frighten her into admitting things she wanted to hear. Could she really be shocked that Judith would be rude to a guy she'd hired to help her do something that bordered on illegal?

Milly struggled to her feet ignoring the throbbing in her head. "You might not know right from wrong," Milly faced her sister. "But I still do." She snatched the bottle out of her sister's hand and offered it to Lucas.

He shook his head. "No. I'm fine. I've had more than enough."

Milly put the bottle back in the pack. The small clearing was blanketed in shadows and the smell of wood rot filled the air. Milly felt like the trees were leaning in, trying to touch her. She wanted to be moving, finding a way out of the forest and into the light.

"I'm not just walking away until I've found Harper." Judith stood with her feet apart, hands on her hips. "Anything could be happening to her."

"Judith," Milly tried to soften her tone. "From what Lucas said, Harper might be near the trail. Heading that way is the best thing to do all round."

Judith unfolded her arms and rubbed her chin. "What about the backpack? Harper's pack?"

"What's she talking about?" Lucas asked looking up at the two women.

Milly explained about finding the shredded pack earlier that morning.

"You were happy to leave the pack and head the other way this morning," Milly pointed out. "You were the one who said it was too dangerous for us to stay and we should head for the trail."

"That was before I found out that my girlfriend has been taken by two strange men."

Milly blinked and tried to keep her mouth from falling open. Even amid all the mayhem, it still threw her to hear her sister calling Harper her girlfriend.

"Milly's right." Lucas started to stand and then staggered to the side. Both women grabbed an arm each and tried to help steady him. "I'm okay, really." He swayed a little but stayed on his feet. "Judith, I think we should head back to the trail."

"But what about the pack?" Judith's eyes were narrowed and her chin tilted up. Milly had seen that look on her sister's face a thousand times when they were kids; it usually meant trouble.

Lucas let out a long breath. "All I know is that the last place I saw her was near the trail, so that's the best place to start looking."

"No. I'm going back to the cliffs. If Harper's there, I'll find her."

Milly wasn't surprised, Judith had always been stubborn – spoiled even. But on the other hand, Harper was Judith's partner; it made sense that she'd do anything to find her. *She's also my best friend*. Milly wondered if that were still true after everything Judith had revealed. Until an hour ago, she'd have sworn she knew Harper inside out, but now it seems the person Milly knew was only a ghost from the past. She realised both Judith and Lucas were looking at her, waiting for her to speak.

"I agree with Lucas, I think we should go back…"

"How can you even contemplate leaving her?" Judith's voice ratcheted up a notch. "She's your best friend and she's in trouble. How can you be so selfish?"

Milly opened her mouth to answer but Judith cut her off. "Don't bother answering. It's clear you're doing this out of spite." Judith took the water bottle out of the bag. "I'm taking the one with a quarter left. There's a full one in the pack."

"You can't seriously be thinking of going off on your own?" Milly reached out to her sister, but Judith stepped away from her. "You heard what Lucas said, there are two men out there capable of God knows what and …" A shaft of pain sliced through Milly skull and all coherent thoughts ceased. Jagged ribbons of colour filled her vision.

"Are you okay?" she was aware of Lucas's deep voice near her face and his arm around her waist, but his words were a confused jumble.

Milly found herself sitting on the ground, a carpet of dry leaves and gum nuts dug into her butt. Judith and Lucas stood over her having a heated discussion as if she weren't there.

"You can see the state she's in. We need to get her out of here as quickly as possible." Lucas jabbed his finger in Milly's direction.

Judith had her arms wrapped around her middle as if she were cold. "I know. I know. That's why I think you should take her back and I'll look for Harper alone."

The pain in Milly's head eased to a heavy thudding. She looked up at the two people standing over her; her vision seemed normal. She blinked her eyes a few times to make sure. She didn't want her sister wandering around alone out in the wilds. The two men Lucas described were the stuff of nightmares; crazed men snatching up women in isolated areas. What was Judith thinking? How could she even contemplate going off alone?

"Please, Jude," Milly spoke up. "Don't go off alone, I can't lose you before we've even had a chance." Exhaustion and pain married together and hit Milly like a slap in the face. All the emotions she'd been trying to control were clamouring for release. Tears flooded her eyes and she could feel her body trembling.

Judith, eyes narrowed, opened her mouth and then closed it again. She dropped to one knee so she was on eye level with her sister. Milly could see the tiny crow's feet at the edge of her startling blue eyes. She looked as exhausted as Milly felt.

"I have to, Mil. She's everything." She put her hand on Milly's knee. Her fingers were cold. "Go with Lucas. You need to get to the hospital."

Judith stood, Milly grabbed her hand. She wanted to tell her to be careful, but it seemed like a stupid warning.

"I pushed him." The words were out. She'd never uttered them to a living soul. Over the last ten years there'd been times when she'd convinced herself the night at the Reach happened just the way she'd told everyone: Drew Crowell jumped in to save Harper. But the truth had always been there gnawing away at everything she touched. She closed her eyes and could see Drew's face. So young, his flawless features drawn back in fear. *No, don't*, his frantic voice in her ear took her breath away. Milly opened her eyes and looked into Judith's.

Judith eyes widened. A look crossed her face, Milly couldn't tell if it was anger or pity. "I know. I've always known ... or guessed."

Now it was Milly's turn to be shocked. "How?"

"Harper. She was on her way up to the top of the Reach when I jumped. She heard Drew cry out." Judith's shoulders sagged. "It wasn't difficult to guess what happened. I know you've been struggling ... battling demons."

"I'm sorry. I'm sorry." Milly's eyes and nose streamed with tears and mucus. "I left you to take all the blame. I'm a coward." Her words came out around hiccupping gasps. "I couldn't jump in and save you that night so I pushed him to ... Then I was too scared to tell the truth."

Judith pulled Milly into an awkward embrace, Judith on one knee and Milly sitting. Milly could smell her sister's hair; it reminded her of their mother's, soft and clean. The secret she'd kept inside eating away at her for ten years was out. There could be no more hiding, no more lying and torturing herself. She'd pictured this moment a thousand times, but in her mind's eye Judith slapped her or screamed accusations. It had never occurred to her she might forgive her.

Judith pulled back. "I was angry with you for a long time, well until yesterday in fact, but ..." She shook her head. "Not anymore." She stood and touched the top of Milly's head, brushing the hair with her finger tips. "I've got to go, Mil. We'll talk when this is over."

"No. It's too dangerous." Milly struggled to her feet and looked for Lucas. He'd moved into the shadows; she couldn't see his face. "Don't let her go." Her voice, high and panicked broke with emotion.

Lucas shook his head, but didn't speak or move to stop her.

"Harper's alive and she needs me." Judith's voice was soft but firm. "I can feel it."

The two women's eyes met: Judith's clear blue and filled with unshed tears, Milly's hazel and red rimmed. A breeze blew through the clearing and ruffled Judith's hair, somewhere in the trees finches chirped. Judith was the first to turn away. She stepped out of the clearing and within a minute vanished into the forest.

Chapter Twenty

Harper felt his presence before she opened her eyes. He was close, his musky smell and the sound of something thudding and sliding against the ground warned her of his proximity. The pain in her arm had subsided to a howl instead of a roar. She suspected the loss of feeling in her injured limb came from the swelling. The thought should have alarmed her, but she felt only gratitude that the agony which drove her to unconsciousness had abated. Slightly.

She was alive. Alive and, as the sound of the wind rustling through the trees and the bird's song told her, still outside. He'd kept her alive just as she knew he would. From the moment this madness began on the way back to the trail, Harper knew what he had in mind for her. Once finished, he'd dispose of her like a used bag of bones. It sickened her, yet after what she'd seen him do to William, part of her just wanted it to happen so the nightmare could end.

She tried to force herself to open her eyes, but the thought of seeing what waited for her sent bursts of fire through her chest. She wanted to curl inward and chase the senseless darkness that had swallowed her only minutes ago. But her mind, now filling with thoughts of knives and blood wouldn't allow her any escape. *If it's my time to die, I'll open my eyes and face it.* Brave thoughts, but still her throat contracted with the pressure of her hammering heart rate.

There was another smell, coppery and pungent. Her mind threw up an image of William, the knife buried in his throat and his eyes wide with helpless terror. Harper gritted her teeth and opened her eyes. The sky had turned from blue to dull-grey. She was on the ground, unyielding and rocky.

Harper turned her head to the left and found the source of the coppery odour. William lay a couple metres away. His head angled towards her, eyes open and misted with a dusty film. She could see the wound in his neck, gaping like a crusty red mouth. He'd been so full of life, his eyes and voice alive with knowledge and kindness. She'd known him only briefly, yet his loss insulted her soul. A flicker of something cold and hard ignited inside her. She'd been running scared for more than twenty-four hours, hiding, screaming, but the sight of William thrown on the ground like a discarded sack changed that. Now a new emotion surged through her like an electrical charge – anger.

Harper raised her head and followed the thumping and scraping sound. She could see his back. He'd taken his black jacket off and underneath wore only a white singlet. He was on his knees. The muscles across his broad shoulders bunched and swelled as he busied himself with his grim task. He was digging; using some sort of small tin spade, the sort of thing campers used to dig latrines.

He's going to bury us, a voice in her head spoke with flat certainty. There would be no more running; her body had given almost all it could. Her only chance was to use what little she had left to stop him before the other one arrived. If she could use the element of surprise, she might be able to overpower him. That would mean she had to act now. Once the other man returned … it would be useless.

Harper waited until his spade struck the earth and curled herself into a sitting position. If she moved carefully, timing each action so that the digging masked her approach, she just might be able to position herself behind him.

The spade struck again and Harper rolled onto her knees. Then with another strike, she made it to her feet. The effort of standing caused her stomach to churn with hunger and fear. Her legs felt like clay, heavy and unresponsive. She scanned the ground for something, anything, to use against him.

Her eyes landed on a pinkish granite rock about the size of a small melon. It looked like the rock had been knocked loose from the ground when he threw William's body down. She fixed her gaze on his back and sidestepped towards William's feet. When his spade hit dirt, Harper stooped and grabbed the rock using her uninjured hand. Her fingers gripped the rough surface, but its weight was too much for her to shift using only one hand. *He's nearly done, it's now or never.*

Harper dragged her eyes away from her tormentor's back and searched for a weapon she could manage. She located another rock, not as big or heavy, a metre or so to her right. It wasn't as deadly looking as the first one. *You'll just have to hit him harder,* her inner voice now active, seemed to be full of advice. *Yes, I'll have to put all my weight into it.*

His movements were slowing down. Either he was growing tired or the grave was almost ready. She waited. *Thump*, sidestep. *Thump*, bend and grab. The rock had some weight to it. Not as much as she'd have liked, but there was a jagged point on the top. If she brought it down in the right spot … *the base of his neck*, the voice in her head sounded excited. Harper could feel her heart jackhammering her ribcage. Her hands trembled. She knew she had to act while she had a burst of adrenalin coursing through her.

She stepped forward, timing her movements like a bridesmaid walking down the aisle. *It'd be funny if there wasn't a dead man a few metres behind me and a lunatic digging my grave,* she thought as she closed in on her target.

His head bobbed and moved from side to side as if surveying his work. Harper stopped moving forward and tried to remain motionless. If he turned, she'd be spotted immediately. The urge to run bubbled up and her feet itched inside her battered hiking boots. *You'll never make it*, the voice whispered, *you're too weak*. Then, *Kill him, it's your only chance*. Harper nodded and kept her eyes trained on the back of his head.

He lifted his head and dug the shovel into the dirt. She stepped forward and almost stumbled on a fallen branch. If not for the noise cover of the shovel hitting the dirt, he'd have heard her boots slipping. Shaken, but undeterred, she moved closer. She could hear his breathing, heavy and guttural.

One more step and she be close enough. When the shovel hit the loose dirt, Harper took the final step. She pulled her arm back, much like a pitcher about to throw. Even as she wound up for the hit, she could feel her left arm lacked the strength needed to make it a killer blow.

Harper swung the chunk of granite with as much force as she could muster and the jagged edge struck home right in the patch of coarse dark hair on the back of his neck. There was a crunching sound as rock sliced flesh and hit bone. He let out a croak and stumbled forward into the shallow pit. Harper, still clutching the rock, crouched and jumped into the pit, almost landing on the back of his legs.

"What the fuck?" Outrage changed the pitch of his voice from deep to high and petulant.

He wrapped a hand around the patch of split skin on the back of his neck and pulled his knees forward. If she hesitated and let him get to his feet, he'd kill her. Of that, she had no doubt. Harper leaned forward, half bending over him, she raised her arm again. Before she struck, he turned his face and looked over his shoulder. The vacuous look she'd seen when he killed William was replaced by terror. His eyes were wide and the pock marks on his cheeks looked angry and red.

"I'll kill y…"

Harper smacked the rock into the base of his skull. There came a sound like Velcro being torn open and the skin on his neck split in a vicious slash of shredded skin and exposed tissue. The blow reverberated up her arm with bone-jarring force. He continued to move, his arms grabbing at the dusty soil, his legs struggling for purchase. Harper felt her stomach contract and hot bile spewed from her mouth. The foul-smelling frothy mess landed between his legs.

For a second, she stood caught between the desire to finish him and the urge to flee and put the sight of his gaping flesh as far behind her as possible. The chunk of granite felt leaden and her arm ached from the blows she'd rained down on him. Still floundering, she didn't catch the change in his posture.

His legs drew up and before she could react, he was on one knee. The metal shovel concealed by his body, swung around and caught her in the chest. Harper felt the air sweep out of her lungs in a hot rush. Something inside her snapped and she toppled to the side. *I'm in my grave*, she thought as her breath wheezed out through her mouth. Her eyes locked on the sky, dark clouds gathered overhead blocking the blue and plunging the afternoon into dimness.

Chapter Twenty-One

Judith moved with urgency, stepping around forest debris and between tightly-packed trees. Keeping her breathing even and her chin up, she pushed her body to keep a brisk pace. She considered herself to be in good shape, and without her sister to slow her down she aimed to be back at the cliff site in less than an hour. Her thoughts were constantly shifting between Milly and Harper.

I pushed him. Those were the words Milly used. After all the years of not knowing, suspecting, she'd finally admitted what really happened. Judith had lived so long with blame and bitterness, it should have been difficult to let go of the anger. But none of it mattered anymore. *If we ever get out of here, no*, she corrected herself. *When we get out of here, I'm going to help my sister forgive herself.* The important thing now was finding Harper.

Leeuwin-Naturaliste National Park is an endless expanse of rugged terrain dominated by steep rocks and dense bush and forest. Finding Harper might be almost impossible, but the torn pack gave Judith a place to start. She had no real way of knowing if she was even headed in the right direction. Her plan now was to backtrack and keep checking the treetops on her left. When the cliff came into view, she'd make a bee-line for it. *That's if I'm not wandering in circles.* She pushed the doubts away; second guessing herself would achieve nothing.

The light changed. Circles of sunshine became patches of grey. Judging by the snatches of sky that appeared above the trees, rain was coming. In this part of the National Park, the ground tended to be coarse and slippery with rotting leaves. Mossy growths covered fallen trees and stumps, filling the air with a damp musty odour. Judith felt the warmth leave the air and shrugged deeper into the fleecy hoodie she'd borrowed from her sister.

Her mind turned back to Milly. Maybe with Lucas to guide her, they'd made it back to the trail. They might be getting close to finding help. Without thinking, she glanced up; seeing only the soupy grey sky, she reminded herself it was too soon to hope for a rescue helicopter. *Still, within the next few hours it might be possible*, her thoughts shifted from despair to hope so swiftly she almost laughed.

She stole another look at the sky and spotted a dark outline that seemed at odds with the treetops. A burst of excitement flared in her stomach and she picked up her pace. With her eyes fixed on the jagged shape of the cliff, Judith let her attention wander. In seconds, her boot caught a narrow root and the world tilted forward.

The impact of the fall slapped the wind out of her lungs and sent her sprawling onto her stomach and chest, mashing the plastic water bottle against her body. Her legs, bare up to the thighs struck the ground. After the initial shock, she pushed herself up onto her knees and brushed at the layer of damp leaves stuck to her jacket.

"Fuck." It came out as more of a moan than a curse.

Judith slumped back onto her butt and shoved the mangled water bottle aside. She examined her knees. Grazed skin coated with dirt. The shock of falling left her feeling rattled. She patted her front right pocket and felt the reassuring bulge of the penknife. Thinking of the knife set her mind on a course she'd been trying to avoid. *What did they do to Harper?* Would she ever find her or would she, like so many other victims of crime in Australia, simply vanish?

Thoughts of Ivan Milat, the notorious serial killer responsible for seven known murders in the 1990s, filled her mind. Judith remembered watching a documentary about the crimes and how Milat had stabbed, shot and beaten his victims. Their bodies were later discovered in the Belanglo State Forest in New South Wales. Leeuwin-Naturaliste National Park was a huge area made up of dense bush and rugged coastal land. In this remote area, the National Park abutted the Boranup Karri Forest; maybe the two men were using the park like Milat had used Belanglo – as a hunting ground. Judith covered her face with her hands trying to block the images that flashed behind her eyes.

The surrounding trees suddenly seemed huge, towering over her and casting a spider's web of shadows wherever she looked. Harper could be anywhere, what hope did Judith have of finding her in the endless kilometres of wilderness? And the penknife, what good would it be against two men crazy enough to abduct a woman in broad daylight? The sense of certainty she'd felt when she left Milly and Lucas ebbed out of her body, leaving her weak and exhausted.

On some level, Judith realised she was overwhelmed and most likely suffering from mild dehydration and exposure, but insight didn't help her shaking hands and panicky thoughts. She snatched up the water bottle, drained the last mouthful, then discarded the container. *Great, now I'm a litter bug*, a silly thought under the circumstances, the sort of thing Harper would have found hilarious. Judith felt a tremor start somewhere deep down and threaten to swallow her up with grief. *Stop it*, she warned herself. *Harper's not dead. No*, she thought, *she's alive and she needs me.*

Judith stood and checked the angle of the cliff. If she kept heading left, she'd run into the area where Milly fell. She tried not to think about what might happen if the two men found her. For all Judith knew, she could be walking towards her own death. Something fluttered in her chest and the urge to turn and run gripped her. Her breath came in sharp pants. In spite of the chill in the air, her hands were slick with sweat. She rubbed them on the front of her shorts and moved on. Slowly, softening the impact of her boots, Judith approached the cliff making as little noise as possible.

Something thumped the ground and she caught movement out of the corner of her eye. Judith gasped and turned to her right. Nothing but trees, bush grass, and shrubs. Holding her breath, she scanned the grey and green thicket. Still keeping her eyes on the trees, she fumbled in her pocket and pulled out the knife.

She swallowed and licked her lips. With her eyes wide and jumping from tree to tree, it took her brain an extra few seconds to acknowledge what it saw. First one kangaroo, then a second. A long shaky breath slipped past her half-open mouth. No more than six metres away the two roos regarded her with curiosity. The smaller of the two, probably a female, continued to chew while the large grey male stood motionless. His heavily muscled shoulders tensed, ready to attack or flee.

The moment stretched and both Judith and the kangaroos waited. Under different circumstances, she'd have probably been enchanted, but all she felt was relief and an underlying sense of annoyance. The blood still pumping in her ears, she shoved the knife back in her pocket and turned away. Her movement startled the creatures and she heard them jump away.

In less than ten minutes, the bush thinned and the trees gave way to an open patch of bush grass. Judith, still trying to remain stealthy in her approach to the cliffs, hesitated. She leaned her weight against a peppermint tree and tried to take in every angle. With no trace of movement, she stepped out into the open.

The patch of open ground directly below the cliff was immediately familiar. Judith threw a quick glance over her shoulder and walked forward. She spotted the remains of the fire she'd built. *Was that only last night?* It seemed an eternity since she and Milly had sat in front of the fire in the dying light.

Judith approached the charred remains and nudged them with the toe of her boot. There were a few remnants of the night the sisters had spent in the area. Judith spotted Milly's watch half buried under leaves and the dusty ground. She picked it up and examined the face. The glass was cracked, probably from Milly's fall, the hands stuck at 3:20. She rubbed her fingers over the band trying to wipe away some of the grime, but only succeeded in making it worse. Finally, she gave up and put the watch in her pocket with the knife.

All this started when their mother died and Judith had the idea to get Milly to confess to what really happened. She looked up at the dark shape of the cliff. *No. It all started at the Reach.* It seemed like her whole life had been lived in the shadow of that place. How could one night … one stupid action, keep causing so much misery? Maybe that was the way God or Karma or whatever worked, by forcing the guilty to carry the weight of their sins – forever.

Judith looked into the ashes left by the fire. "I can do that … I can carry the weight of it, just as long as you don't take Harper away from me," she realised she was speaking aloud, praying. She swallowed and wiped her eyes. She'd never believed in God. But the idea of a caring creator felt comforting. She could understand why people turned to religion in times of stress. Here she was, an atheist, crying and praying to a God she didn't believe existed until five minutes ago. Even so, voicing her thoughts made her feel less alone. *If you are listening*, she hesitated, feeling a bit self-conscious, *help me find her.* Judith looked up at the darkening sky. Streaks of stark light beaming through heavy storm clouds somehow terrifying and breath-taking at the same time. She had to move now, before the National Park was awash.

A semi-circle of trees arched the clearing. When Milly found the pack, she'd been in a thick swatch of trees and bushes. Judith frowned and scanned the edges of the forest. She could see little to distinguish one crop of trees from the next. Remembering the exact location of the pack might be more difficult than she thought.

The sky rumbled as if getting ready to unleash its fury. Judith bit her bottom lip and tried to think. She remembered watching Milly walk into the trees, the way she limped to the right. "Which way?" Judith turned left then back to the right.

She ran her hands through her hair and closed her eyes. *Okay, now's the time for some divine intervention,* Judith thought and opened her lids. The first thing she noticed were the boot prints in the dusty earth. It had obviously been days since it last rained because the ground was just dry enough for their footprints to be visible.

The area around the fire had been heavily trampled and near the cliff, long smooth patches of sand showed the outline of where the two women slept. Judith stepped around the fire, eyes trained on the ground. Even in the dimness, she could make out her boot prints leading towards the ashes. Crouching forward, she spotted two sets leading off to the left.

"Yes." She broke into a jog and followed the prints into the trees.

The tightly-packed trunks and thick canopy blocked most of what little light remained. Judith thought of the torch and cursed herself for not thinking to take it from Milly's pack. She waited on the edge of the clearing. After a minute or so, her eyes began to adjust to the gloom. A gust of wind pushed at her back as if trying to move her deeper into the wilderness.

A few metres in, Judith noticed a patch of watery light shining through a small clearing. The area looked familiar, but everything in the National Park looked so similar it was difficult to tell one place from the next. A few shoulder-high grey bushes edged the tiny patch. Upon closer inspection, she could see the weeds to the right of the bushes had been trampled. Standing on the crushed growth, Judith turned and surveyed the clearing.

The pack hung from a low-lying branch, one shoulder strap trailing down like a broken limb. Judith's first impulse was to rush forward and grab the backpack, but then another thought occurred to her. She'd spotted the tracks, maybe whoever left the pack also left behind footprints. She edged her way towards a twisted wattle tree where the torn pack hung.

The wind kicked up another notch shaking the trees and filling the forest with ghostly rattling. Unlike the denser parts of the Leeuwin-Naturaliste National Park, the small clearing was free of the usual carpet of rotting leaves and seed pods. Judith crouched low and studied the ground. Nothing. She worked her way around the tree keeping one hand on the coarse trunk. Behind the wattle, a crop of native shrubs similar in appearance to salt bushes, crowded the trunk. She doubted anyone would have pushed their way through the spikey bushes to reach the tree. And if they had, there would be visible depressions or breakage.

Judith circled back around to section of the trunk that faced the clearing. She studied the branch and the surrounding ground, tapping her forefinger on her bottom lip. She could find absolutely no sign of anyone approaching the tree nor any explanation for how the pack ended up swinging from the branch.

Reaching out with her right hand she touched the pack. It felt slick and damp, unpleasant to the touch.

"Harper, where are you?" Judith whispered and rubbed the strap between her thumb and forefinger.

How could the backpack have ended up here without someone putting it in the tree? It didn't make any sense. Things don't just fall out of the sky. Judith's head snapped up. Maybe that's exactly what happened. She gazed up at the swatch of grey overhead. The clouds hung heavy and threatening over the clearing with weak tears of light struggling to push through the gloom. She pulled the pack down. The nylon felt slippery, it made her think of snake skin. She swallowed and rummaged through the pack hoping to find water or food. Apart from a crumpled muesli bar, the pack was empty. She studied the snack bar for a moment. Nutty Cluster, Harper's favourite. Her chin trembled. She blinked away tears that threatened to form and tore the wrapper open. The sweet smell of nuts and honey made her stomach groan and her mouth fill with saliva. Judith ate the bar in two bites then licked the paper. When she'd finished, she stared at the wrapper clenched in her grubby hand and a pang of disgust hit her. Judith dropped the pack and the sticky wrapper. She turned away and jogged back to the cliff, the hood of her jacket bobbing up and down against her back.

When she reached the base of the cliff, she stood back and gazed up at the ragged outline. If someone had been standing at the top, someone with a strong enough arm, he could have hurled the pack into the trees. She felt a burst of excitement. It was more than possible that Harper could still be up there somewhere and the pack only ended up down in the trees because someone threw it.

She had two choices. The first, walk back through the forest and come around the cliff. That way would take her anywhere up to three hours. Or, the second option, scale the cliff and make it to the top in maybe fifteen minutes. *Or fall and break my neck*, Judith thought and pictured the moment her sister fell and hit the ground with a sickening thump. Only yesterday Milly had taken a terrifying fall while trying to climb down, could she really be considering climbing up without any gear?

She tried to sort through the possibilities. Backtracking to the point where she'd left Lucas and Milly would take valuable time. Harper had been missing in the National Park for over twenty-four hours. The men might have even taken her and headed into the Boranup Forest. She didn't know where one area ended and the other began, only that it would be easy to dispose of someone in such immense wilderness. Could she really waste another three hours playing it safe? But if she tried to climb the cliff and fell, she'd not only be injured and alone, there'd be no one to look for Harper until the police arrived.

Distant thunder rumbled ominously as if warning her to hurry. The wind icy and fresh lifted her hair. She shivered and pulled the hoodie's zip up to her throat. She could smell the rain gathering in the air. If she intended to climb, she'd have to do it now before the rain started and the wind picked up.

She searched the rock face looking for an area that offered some ease of climbing. On the far right, the rock sloped backwards and after the first three metres or so, there were a series of ridges and shelves that might offer the safest way up. She'd take a chance and climb.

Her hands were damp with sweat. She rubbed them on her shorts, then placed them on the rock. The cold granite sent chills up her arms. Reaching up, she found an indent and began pulling herself up. She'd been climbing with Harper many times. Mostly at indoor facilities but a few times outdoors. Heights didn't bother her, or at least they never had in the past. But then again, she'd never climbed solo without a harness or bilayer.

By the time she was a few metres off the ground, Judith felt the first patter of rain hit the top of her head. She saw the dark spots appear on the dusty surface of the rock and felt the wind slap at her face. She reached the top of the first slope and leaned her body against the flat rock, mashing her breasts and stomach flat on the cold granite. With her face turned to the side, she managed to look up and find a secure-looking edge. With her fingers crimped to keep her hand closer to the rock, she used a bridging motion to apply equal pressure with her hands and feet in opposite directions. Her body slid upward, thighs scraping the rock face.

Another upward sweep and she found purchase in a bucket large enough for her whole hand. She raised her right leg and pressed her boot against a jagged outcrop. Her body now spread wide, her muscles quivered with the strain. She focused on keeping her breathing even and pushing upwards. The rain continued to spit fat drops on her head and face.

Now nearly at the halfway mark, wind blustered her bare legs and ice-cold rain splattered her cheeks. Her teeth felt numb like blocks of ice, her lips cracked and glued to her gums. She had the urge to scratch her nose. She ignored it and clung to the rock. One more push and she reached a mantle about fifteen centimetres wide. Using a move similar to getting out of a swimming pool without using steps, Judith hoisted herself up.

Scarcely wide enough for her feet, the mantle gave her a chance to catch her breath and allow her trembling muscles a minute's reprieve. "Nearly there," she spoke through gritted teeth, her fingers curled into tiny cracks in the granite.

The constant patter of fat raindrops worked its way through her hoodie and shorts until everything she wore felt damp against her skin. She craned her neck trying not to lean out. Only five metres or so until she reached the top, but the thought of leaving the mantle and grappling for footing became more terrifying with every passing second. *If I don't move, I'll hang here until I lose strength in my arms and legs and drop,* she warned herself. Yet still her body refused to move. *This must be what Milly felt like,* Judith realised. *She was this afraid and I told her to climb down knowing she'd fall.* She pushed the thought away and forced her fingers to uncurl and reach up. Driving upwards with her right leg, she hooked her hand into a narrow crevice. With her left leg swinging unsupported, she tried to swing sideways and up using her arms and one leg. It was an awkward crab-like jump that ended with both her feet on a narrow crimp and her hands clawing at rubble and swatches of vegetation.

Judith gulped in cold air and clung to the rock. Her fingers were stinging and raw and the tendons in her hands twanged with the effort of clenching so tightly. *Keep moving*, the words repeated over and over in her mind as if there were a direct connection between the thought and her fatigued limbs. A few more moves and she'd be at the top. Only, looking up, the cliff seemed to stretch for miles.

The climbing motion pulled her tattered shirt tail and hoodie, scrunching the clothing up around her ribs. Bitter wind slapped at the small of her back until she felt the cold working its way into her bones. Judith searched above her head first with her right hand and then her left. Finding nowhere to grab, not even a tiny crevice, she had no choice but to make a sideways movement. She turned her head to the right and lay her left cheek against the rough granite. The rain changed from a patter to a drizzle, soft yet cold and constant.

She squinted her eyes and searched for a way forward through sideward movement. Without thinking, she stuck out her tongue and let the rain trickle into her mouth. She spotted a jagged knob a metre or so to her right. Stretching her arm and leaning sideways, she crawled her fingers across the granite until her body leaned at nearly ninety degrees. With her fingers around the small outcrop, she slid her right leg across the rock and found a narrow dip. Hiking boots had thick soles and a chunky design which made them perfect for walking for hours over rough terrain, but almost useless when climbing. She managed to slide the toe of her boot into the dip. Balancing her entire weight on her toes, she inched sideways. Then very slowly, rain dripping from her eyelashes and blurring her vision, she slid her left foot over to the dip.

With both sets of toes balanced on the narrow dip, Judith looked up. Through the drizzle, she could just make out a series of sizable hand jams and outcrops. If she could pull herself up, it would be two easy moves to the top. She pushed down on her toes and strained upwards. Then, pressing down on the outcrop with her right hand, she swung her left up. As the fingers of her left hand curled into a crevice, the outcrop under her right gave way. Her right foot slid out of the narrow dip and skidded downwards. A shower of rubble tumbled past her dangling foot.

Judith croaked out a panicked scream. Her body bounced jarring her chin against the granite. Her heart seemed to vibrate in her ears. For a fraction of a second, the sensation of falling overwhelmed her and she screwed her eyes shut. Grasping the crevice with her left hand and leaning into the rock face on her left foot, she managed to steady herself and control her downward slide.

"Oh God. Oh God." The words tumbled out like a mantra.

Holding her breath, she opened her eyes. The urge to freeze came fast and strong. Judith realized that if she hesitated, she'd quickly become paralysed by fear. Jamming the toe of her right boot back into the narrow dip, she pushed up and found solid purchase on a ridge almost half a meter wide. Within seconds, she found herself standing on the ridge head and shoulders just above the top of the cliff.

She leaned forward onto her stomach then flung her right leg up and rolled over until she lay atop the cliff staring at the dark, menacing sky.

Rain pelted her face and body, filling her mouth with sweet tasting water. Numbness engulfed her. The effort of her chest rising and falling took all her remaining strength.

She had no desire to move or think, yet her mind turned with images of her mother falling, her sister hitting the ground below the cliff and finally, Drew. She didn't see him fall, but her mind threw up gruesome flashes of what his final seconds would have looked like.

She sat up. Her chin stung, absently she pressed the back of her hand to the graze left from hitting the granite. Could everything that had happened be contributed to coincidence? Three people all connected. Drew, Milly and their mother. Two fatal falls and one near miss. It might be possible, but unlikely. She looked at her hand and saw a streak of blood.

Maybe exhaustion and fear were twisting her thinking. Either way, something sinister was at work and the need to find Harper felt stronger than ever. Judith stood, groaning like a senior citizen. With no idea where to go, her only option was to head back to the coast and hope the rain hadn't washed away all traces of Harper and the two men who took her.

Chapter Twenty-Two

"Your mum's had a fall," Harper's voice, husky and solemn, cut through Milly's alcohol-dazed mind.

She'd been asleep. Not asleep, passed out when the phone rang. The shrill ringing melted into her dreams where Drew's face, distorted in terror, loomed over her as she hung from the edge of a knife-shaped black rock. Milly, jolted awake by the phone, gasped out a startled shriek.

With her bedroom still swathed in darkness, she fumbled for the phone. By the time Milly realised what Harper was saying, she'd already stopped speaking. There was silence on the line.

"A fall?" Milly tried to form her jumbled thoughts into words. "Where is she?"

Harper let out a breath. A tired sound somewhere between a sigh and a groan. "She's... she passed away. I'm so sorry, Milly. It must have happened yesterday afternoon. Susan, your mum's cleaning lady found..."

"What? How did she pass away?" Milly pressed the phone against her ear and reached out her other hand to flick on the bedside lamp. A circle of dim yellow light chased away the darkness.

"It looks like she fell down the stairs. I don't know how it happened. The police were there when I spoke to Judith. They think it must have been an accident."

"My mother can't have passed away." Milly now fully awake began to realise what was happening. Her best friend was calling in the middle of the night. No. In Perth it was earlier. *Yes,* Milly thought, *she'd forgotten the time difference.* She picked up her watch from the bedside table; her hand shook.

"Are you there, Milly?" Harper sounded different. Her voice deeper.

"Milly?"

* * *

Lucas's dark eyes bored into hers. Milly blinked and her vision cleared. The light surrounding him, a dim haze, but his features were in sharp focus. She moved her head and realised the buzzing had stopped but the pain remained. "I must have fallen asleep." Milly knew she was laying on the ground, but couldn't remember how she got there. The smell of damp leaves and woody earth hung over her.

"You passed out." Lucas continued to regard her, as if fascinated. "Your nose is bleeding."

Milly touched her nose and felt the warm wetness. She looked at her fingers coated with blood. "Did I fall?" She sat up, pulled the edge of her shirt out of her shorts and wiped her nose.

"No. You just toppled to the side after your sister left." He was hunkered down next to her, his hands dangling between his legs. His face only centimetres away from hers. "I called you a few times, but you were out for the count."

"How long?"

He seemed to be about to say something but changed his mind. "Not long. A few minutes." He stood and picked up her pack. "It's going to rain." He held out his hand for her to take. "We should keep going."

Milly reached out and took his hand. His skin, warm and rough felt good against her cold palm. He pulled her to her feet. She winced and let out a gasp.

"Your head?" he asked, still holding her hand.

"No. Well yes. My head and my back." Milly pulled her hand free and rubbed the back of her head.

Lucas turned and started walking. Milly wiped at her nose again and followed him into the trees. She could feel the moisture in the air, it wouldn't be long before the rain started. Her thoughts turned to Judith. *Maybe we'll reach the trail before she finds Harper ... or those men find her.* Milly didn't want to dwell on what might happen to her sister or what might have already happened to her friend.

Lucas walked ahead of her, head up and shoulders moving. He seemed to know exactly where they were heading. Milly tried to match her pace to his, but her legs seemed to be out of sync with her brain. When they veered left and began heading upwards, Milly felt her chest heaving as if she'd run a marathon.

"I can't keep up this pace." She leaned against a marri tree for support. "I've got to stop and catch my breath."

Lucas stopped walking but didn't turn around. Milly slid down the tree and felt her butt hit the ground with a thump. She turned her body sideways and slumped against the trunk. Lucas stood motionless, his back to her. He seemed to be listening for something. Milly thought of the two men. Maybe he could hear something she couldn't? She didn't blame him for being on edge.

She lifted her head off the tree and looked around. Trees, shrubs and creepers, thinned out now but still no open ground. A bird squawked; a piercing shriek that reminded her of a baby crying. She shuddered and wrapped her arms around her body. She was about to call out to him and ask what he was doing when he turned and his gaze fell on her.

"It won't hurt to take a break," he said as if she'd asked him a question.

He moved back to her and sat down a metre or so away on a hunk of granite. "I always wanted to go camping when I was a kid, but we didn't have the money for gear." He dumped the pack between his legs and fished out the water bottle. "Here." He held the bottle towards her.

Milly frowned and took the bottle. She had to clamp it between her knees to get the top off. She took a sip and handed it back without speaking.

"We never had the money to go away on holidays," he continued. "I was always jealous of other kids who had parents that could take time off work." His voice was low and conversational. "What about you?"

The question startled her as did his sudden talkativeness. "What?"

Lucas took a sip from the bottle and then put it back in the pack. "Did you get to go on holidays when you were a kid?"

The question struck her as strange, then again at least he was trying. "I... we went on holidays." Milly leaned her head against the tree thinking about her mum and dad and the car trips to their holiday house in Busselton. Her and Judith in the back seat playing Uno. Sometimes a song would come on the radio that her dad liked and he'd turn the music up and sing. It always made her mum laugh. That sound, her mum's laughter. Milly realised she'd never hear it again and a sob caught in her throat.

"What did you say?" His words jolted her.

Milly's eyes snapped open. She hadn't realised she'd closed them. "Sorry, Lucas. I was just thinking about my mother." She swallowed. "What were you saying?"

"We should get moving. Are you ready?" He stood over her and swung the pack onto his shoulder. "A storm's coming."

Milly looked up at the sky. Clouds gathering above looked dark and threatening. She thought about hiking in the rain and wished for comfort. A warm bed, clean clothes. It seemed like she'd been in this place for an eternity and the weariness that consumed her felt like a physical weight draped over her body.

She pushed up with her knees and steadied herself against the tree. Lucas was already on the move, his boots crunching over the carpet of forest debris that seemed to cloak every inch of the park. A moment ago, he'd been trying to engage her, open up. Now he'd fallen back into mute indifference. Not that she cared. All she could think of now was Judith and Harper. *And* getting out of the wilderness.

Milly followed Lucas as he strode up a steep slope. Trees grew at strange sideways angles as if they were using their roots to pull themselves up the incline. Lucas appeared unimpeded by the climb, head up and legs moving in confident measured steps. Milly on the other hand had to walk bent over, her hands almost trailing across the rocks and dusty ground.

By the time she reached the top, Lucas had moved farther away from her. His gait swift and urgent. Milly stumbled after him, her mouth open and gasping for breath.

"Lucas, wait." If he heard her calling, he gave no indication.

His black shirt disappeared into a scattering of trees. Her heart jumped into her mouth. She lurched towards the trees, her mind racing with questions. *Why would he leave her? What made him act so strangely?* Overriding the questions grew a fear of being left alone and defenceless in the forest.

Milly reached the trees just as the rain began to fall. A light pattering of drops settled on her hair and shoulders. She pushed through the trees and found herself fighting against shrubs and branches. The scrub tore at her clothes and hair. She stumbled forward.

"Lucas? Lucas, where are you?" Her voice sounded thin and tremulous.

She paused and listened. The only sound, raindrops tapping leaves and bark on their way to the ground. Milly scanned the tangle of trees and bushes. She could see no sign of him and no indication as to which way he'd gone. It made no sense. Had he decided she was too much of a liability and taken off? Surely he wouldn't just abandon her. But again, she realised she knew nothing about him.

Alone, her only option was to keep heading up towards the trail. That had to be where Lucas was going. Even if she couldn't catch up with him, at least she might eventually run into other hikers. Part of her wanted to give in to exhaustion and stop, but she kept coming back to Judith, touching her hair. *We'll talk when this is over*, that's what she'd said before walking into the forest alone. Milly had to keep going. Judith needed her to get help and that's what she intended to do.

Feeling more certain than she had in years. Milly forced her feet to move. With or without Lucas's help, she'd find her way out of this crazy maze of forest and rocks. The rain fell in a constant drizzle, soaking her shirt and chilling her skin. Milly swiped at her face with the back of her hand and noticed blood. Her nose had started bleeding again.

She'd been walking for about five minutes when the she felt the wilderness thin and the spaces between vegetation grow wider. She spotted a small clearing, gloomy and laced with shadows. A branch creaked and something shuffled out of view.

"Lucas?" Milly stepped into the clearing and turned her head left and right. The movement sent shivers of pain running over her scalp.

She could hear the blood pumping in her ears and her breath, sharp and short. She turned back the way she'd entered and Lucas was standing between her and the trees.

The rhythm of her heart changed and she let out a gasp. Frightened and then relieved, she stepped towards him. "I couldn't keep up with you." The words tumbled out. "I thought I'd lost you."

"I just wanted to scout ahead, make sure we were going the right way." His voice was little more than a whisper. "Your nose is bleeding."

Milly swiped at her upper lip knowing her hand would come away bloody. She wanted to ask if they could stop for a few minutes, but didn't know how he'd take the request. The way he'd taken off ahead of her made Milly think he'd grown sick of having to babysit her.

"You should sit down for a minute and take a break." The sudden kindness surprised her. It was the last thing she expected him to say.

She looked around for a place to rest. Sitting close to the trees offered the best protection from the drizzling rain. Lucas still stood at the edge of the clearing so instead of sitting near him, she chose a tree on the far edge and crouched beneath it.

Lucas waited for her to be settled and then moved over and sat next to her. Thunder rumbled overhead and the rain intensified. The thought of being out in the wilds during a storm made Milly shiver.

"Are you cold?"

"No. Well, yes a bit but it's the thunder..." Milly turned to look at him and her vision clouded. The buzzing in her ears returned, this time piercing in its intensity. Without thinking, she clapped her hands over her ears and gasped.

"Something wrong?" His voice sounded hollow as if he were speaking from the end of a tunnel.

Milly tried to shake her head, but the slightest movement sent spirals of agony through her brain. She sank onto her butt and lowered her head onto her knees. She felt his hand on her back, warm and strong. Milly clamped her teeth together and tried to will the pain away.

After what seemed like five minutes, but was more likely ten seconds, the buzzing ebbed and the pain receded to a more bearable thumping. She let out a long puff of air and raised her head.

"Sorry," she didn't know what else to say. "My head. It's been bothering me since the fall. I must be concussed or something."

Lucas's face remained blank, unreadable. If he felt concerned or worried, it didn't show. His dark, almost black eyes regarded her as if she were something strange and unusual. Milly felt the blood rushing to her cheeks and turned away. He was attractive in a rough sort of way, but something about him left her feeling nervous and off balance.

"When I was a teenager," he began as if Milly hadn't mentioned her concerns about having a head injury. "I thought I was the only person in the world who knew what it was like to be all alone."

Milly became very aware of his hand on her back. His closeness made her uncomfortable. If she got up and moved it would be very obvious, almost rude. She thought about suggesting they start walking again, but her legs felt numb and her back had finally stopped aching. She wanted to rest for a few more minutes.

"I bet you've never had to feel like that?" He waited, as if expecting some sort of answer. Unsure of what to say, Milly looked down at her lap and remained silent.

"I was in a foster home. Did you know that?"

Milly didn't like the way his voice changed. The words were laced with anger. The pressure of his hand on her back increased. His fingers dug into the fabric of her shirt.

"I think we should get going," Milly tried to keep the tremor out of her voice. She moved to stand but his fingers pulled on her shirt and she toppled back losing her balance and falling against him.

"I thought you needed a rest?" There was no trace kindness in his words, only ice. He held her against him, his hand slipping around her back and circling her waist.

Hindered by the binding around her middle and the pounding in her head, Milly felt panic rising in her like a tornado. Her mind reeled with frightening possibilities. Pressed against his side, she could feel his muscular torso and the heat coming from him. There was also an element of embarrassment and confusion. She wondered if she might be misreading the situation, the panic she felt just an overreaction.

"Did you, Milly?" he persisted.

"Did I what?" Milly asked around a quick intake of breath. She didn't want to say the wrong thing and make the situation worse. *The situation is way past worse.*

"Did you know I was in a foster home?" He spoke each word slowly, in a flat impatient tone as if speaking to a difficult child.

Milly bit her lip and the cut from yesterday's fall opened up. She searched her mind for the right reply, but could think of nothing. Lucas gave her an impatient shake. It was only a small movement, but she could feel the power.

"I... I didn't know." She stuttered out the answer hoping he'd be satisfied and turn her lose. The change in his behaviour terrified her. She'd been around men who changed when they drank. When she was hospitalised for depression, there'd been men who had problems with anger, but nothing like this. It occurred to her that maybe she was seeing the real Lucas for the first time. She thought of Judith's words, *we barely know him. And* he had agreed to Judith and Harper's scheme to get her out here and frighten her. For all she knew, Lucas could be capable of anything.

"No. You've had a pretty sweet life. You and your sister." He spun on his toes and pushed her down onto her butt so he was crouched over her. "You wouldn't know what it's like to be alone and powerless." He squeezed her shoulders, his fingers biting into her skin.

She gasped. "Not until now." His eyes looked huge and shiny.

Milly wriggled backwards on her butt and pushed at his chest. His shirt tore, revealing the skin underneath. She saw his chest and sucked in air as if jolted by an electric shock. She pulled her eyes away from what the bare skin revealed and met his gaze.

"Surprise," he said without a trace of humour.

Chapter Twenty-Three

Judith jogged across the open ground taking care to avoid a misstep on the chunks of granite peppering the landscape. The rain fell in sharp fingers, not yet a downpour, but enough to blur her vision and chill her skin. The volley of water darkened the rocks from pink to almost red. Judith felt she was getting close. It wasn't something she could put her finger on, just a growing sensation of dread.

Something else danced around the edges of her thoughts clamouring for attention. A sense that she'd missed something. Something of vital importance. *Find Harper,* that was her priority.

She glanced up at the sky. The light was dying around her, the approaching storm bringing a premature darkness to the late afternoon. Surely Lucas and Milly had at least reached the trail. She'd had to backtrack for over an hour to reach the cliff. Then it had taken her a good twenty minutes to climb to the top. That gave the others a huge head start.

Another thought crept into her mind. What if Milly's head injury is worse than they thought? Maybe she'd collapsed. Judith stopped jogging and bent over with her hands on her knees. She sucked in air and tried to hold back the worry building up inside her. She kept hearing the sound her sister's head made when she hit the ground; kept feeling the sick hollow sensation in her stomach when she'd thought she'd lost her.

Judith straightened up and put her hands on her hips. She was no good to Harper *or* Milly if she let panic overwhelm her. *They could be halfway to the carpark by now.* But a small voice in her head whispered in disagreement, *you don't believe that. No*, she thought. *I don't.* Her gut told her they were all in danger.

Judith looked over her shoulder. Scraggy clumps of salt trees and stony ground sat in silence, save for the distant chatter of birds and wailing of the wind. The uninhabited wilderness took on an eerie quality. Alone and fighting panic, it was easy to imagine things moving and shifting just beyond her plane of vision. She turned her attention forward and tried to shake off the feeling that something sinister was creeping up on her. *I'm just spooked.* "Is it any wonder?" she said aloud.

Moving on, the landscape changed. Salt trees ranging from waist high bushes to towering grey mini-trees grew tightly in some areas and sparsely in others. *I'm getting closer to the coast,* Judith thought and felt a prickle of fear. In truth, Harper could be anywhere, but her gut told her, she was near. But near to what, she had no idea.

A gust of wind whipped up her damp hair and the smell of seaweed, faint but distinctive filled her nose. She broke into a run eager to reach the trail and hopefully find some trace of her girlfriend. Judith's boots pounded the sodden ground and struck the occasional smooth chunk of granite with a resounding thud. Her soggy clothes clung to her, rasping and chafing with each step.

The soughing of the ocean told her she was heading in the right direction. Judith forced herself to stop and draw breath. The rocks were slippery, if she kept running it would only be a matter of time before she fell. Despite the wintry freshness of the wind, sweat ran in warm lines down her back. Judith allowed herself a minute or so to catch her breath. She looked up at the sky and poked out her tongue, lapping up drops of water like a thirsty dog. It wasn't much, just a thin trickle of moisture, but it felt good on her parched lips.

Ready to move on, she happened to look left. The rain saturated, the ground tinting the sand a muddy orange. It struck her that she was looking at a patch of ground where the red leaked onto the sand. Judith frowned and for a second felt only confusion. Then realisation flared in her mind. It wasn't the colour leaching out of the granite – that would be impossible. The ground was stained with blood.

As her mind processed what her eyes saw, Judith gagged and clamped her hand over her mouth. She became acutely aware of the blood beating in her ears, it eclipsed all other sound. *Harper?* Her mind threw up images of her girlfriend laying on the couch in fleecy pyjamas, standing over the stove stirring pasta sauce – all the simple mundane things she took for granted. All washed away in a puddle of blood.

She took a step closer trying to breathe through her mouth and keep the smell of death out of her nostrils. Everywhere her gaze landed, more blood. The rocks were splattered with dark stains made streaky by the rain. *So much blood.* Her mind wanted to shut down and disallow the certainty that no one could survive losing that much lifeblood.

A tremor started deep in Judith's body and spread through her like fire. All the fear and exhaustion of the last twenty-four hours seemed unimportant, trivial. Her body jerked forward and a guttural sob tore through her throat. She clenched her fists together and jammed them against her mouth. Harper's face, lit up with mischief, flashed in her mind. A woman of limitless kindness, butchered. Judith's mind reeled with thoughts of the terror and pain

Harper must have felt. The rain drove through her clothes and plastered her hair to her face. She shivered, not from the cold but from sobs that wracked her body. *This is my fault*, she thought bitterly. Harper never wanted to push Milly into admitting the truth. If Judith hadn't talked her into it, she'd still be alive. The guilt felt like a physical weight pushing her down.

Time passed, she didn't know how much. Eventually the sobs turned to sniffing and she became aware of the cold. She forced herself upright. The landscape seemed changed, dull. As if Harper's absence from the world lessened it somehow. Judith jammed her palms into her eyes, rubbing the rain and tears away.

"I should have been with you." She was barely aware of her own voice. "You must have been so scared." As she spoke her gaze settled on the bloody ground. Rivers of crusty sand were rapidly dissipating under the force of the rain. The trail of sand and blood no match for the building storm.

Judith frowned and sniffed. Twin gouges in the sand coloured almost black with blood. The marks led away from the scene. Judith held her breath to avoid smelling the thick coppery odour and crouched down. The tracks were clearly visible as they cut through the mess on the sand. For five metres or so, blood filled most of the indentation then the trail continued away.

She stood and picked her way through the grisly mess. The rain intensified and the marks began to blur. Hurrying now, Judith made her way beside the rivulets. Pausing to search for traces of Harper's presence, she spotted more marks. Some too faint, but a few, clearly boot prints of varying sizes. Judith was no tracker, but she knew what she was seeing. Two people had been through this area. One big and one small. Not only that, but a body had been dragged away from the bloody scene towards a snatch of salt bushes.

Judith's heart fluttered. Could it be possible that there had been a third person? Maybe the body wasn't Harper's but someone else's. Even as she allowed herself hope, part of her mind resisted, telling her the chances of another person being involved were slim.

"A slim chance is better than none," she said through chattering teeth, and took off towards the trees.

The greyish-green trunks with patchy foliage were at least two metres high. Judith slowed down as she approached. *There are two men*, she reminded herself. Could the smaller boot prints be from one of them? *No.* She decided the second set of marks were either made by a child or a woman. Her gut told her it was a woman.

The salt trees formed a natural arc, creating a pathway flanked by narrow tree trunks. Overhead sporadic branches formed a sparse shelter. The whole effect reminded Judith of a giant rib cage, like something out of a palaeontology museum. Stepping into the tunnel of trees, the weak grey light outside plummeted to shadowy gloom.

Judith pulled the knife from her pocket and worked the blade open. A damp oaky smell hung in the air. The ground was dark, the colour of a muddy pond. She narrowed her glance, focusing on the ground. She looked for any signs a body had been dragged this way, but without the light, the marks criss-crossing the dirt looked like a network of gouges. Being inside the trees made her feel trapped and vulnerable. If the men were lying in wait, they could enter one from each end and she'd be surrounded.

A hollow sensation in the pit of her stomach threatened to explode into full-blown terror. She focused on her breathing, listening to the raspy sound as her boots scuffed through the dirt. If her gut instinct was right and Harper did come this way, there might be a chance she was still alive. The thought of reliving the desolation she'd felt when it seemed certain Harper was dead, frightening her more than whatever the two men might do to her. At least that's what she told herself to keep her feet moving.

When she finally broke free of the trees, Judith ducked to the right and crouched against the edge of the greenery. The area in front of her opened up onto a landscape similar to that near the trail: dusty ground dotted with salt bushes and chunks of pink granite. The rain faltered but didn't quite stop. She spotted a patch of colour at odds with the greys, pinks, and greens of the landscape. She squinted and then flicked away the drops of rain that hung on her eyebrows. A piece of red fabric poked out from the base of a small salt bush.

Judith hesitated. After a quick look around, she stood and walked the ten or so metres. The fabric turned out to be a hat. She picked it up and felt the damp cloth. It was an odd-looking thing with a flap at the rear. It could have been dropped by anyone and sat out in the bush for weeks. But if that were the case, surely the colour would be faded and the fabric dirty. She turned the hat over in her hands. It had some stains, but they looked fresh and the red too vivid to have been bleached by the sun.

A few metres farther on, near a small crop of what looked like peppermint trees, an irregular mound became visible. It lay just out of Judith's visual range making it difficult for her to identify, but from a distance it looked dark – a sprawled human shape. A cold finger of fear ran up her neck. The wind kicked up a notch and the shape rippled. Instinctively, she swivelled her head around searching for signs of the two men. Seeing nothing but wilderness on all sides, she moved closer.

With each step the shape coalesced until it clearly became a body slumped on the ground. She gripped the handle of the knife. It felt slippery with sweat. All sorts of possibilities flooded her mind. At the forefront, the desperate fear that the body could be Harper. *No*, she thought. *It can't be her.* She repeated the thought over and over as she moved closer on legs that felt disconnected from her body.

Ten metres out from the body, Judith let out a deep shuddering breath. The shape was too large to be Harper. No sooner had relief come, then her cheeks flushed with guilty heat. The body *was* a human being. Still, the realisation that her girlfriend might still be alive made her pick up her pace.

The smell hit her first. Thick and pungent, a too sweet odour. Not until she saw the man's milky eyes and the gaping wound on his neck did she recognise the smell as something the body emits in death. Her hand flew to her neck and her mouth filled with saliva. The urge to vomit almost overwhelmed her.

"Oh God." Judith felt herself sway. She tried to look away but couldn't drag her gaze from the man's eyes.

Time passed. She wasn't sure how long she stood there wanting to run, but incapable of moving. Bits of information began to make it past the shock and repulsion. The man was clearly elderly; his hair, sparse and white reminded her of fairy floss. His legs were long and thin, sticking out of baggy blue shorts. Her eyes drifted down to his feet. For some reason, the red socks cut through the numbness and brought a flood of tears. She imagined the poor old man putting his socks on this morning. Maybe they were his favourite. Maybe his wife bought them for him. Had he any idea this would be his last day on earth?

Judith lifted her hand to wipe her nose and realised she still held the red hat. She took a step towards the body and bent over. Not sure why, she felt the need to return the hat to its owner.

"I'm sorry." The words came out in a rush. The wind ruffled the dead man's fairy floss hair. Using her left hand, she sat the hat on the man's shoulder.

A rattling sound broke through the patter of the rain. It sounded like pebbles or rocks scattering. Judith straightened and whipped her head around. The possibility that she wasn't alone hit her for the first time since coming upon the body. The shock of finding a dead man, especially one killed with such violence, had swept away all thoughts of the two men that most likely committed the crime. Now, Judith became acutely aware of her situation.

The sodden hoodie clung to her and chilled her skin. She held the knife out in front of her as if expecting an attack. She stood in an open space where the ground sloped upwards at a slight angle. To her left salt bushes and sporadic crops of trees; ahead lay open ground and rocks for fifteen or so metres, then snatches of trees and shrubs. It was easy to imagine someone waiting, watching. Judith stood motionless and listened. If someone *was* lurking out of sight, her only chance would be to hear his movements. She tensed her body hoping to pick up any sound over the volley of water. Standing in the rain next to a dead body, her instincts screamed for her to run.

After what felt like minutes, she began to relax her arm and lower the knife. Another patter of pebbles came and then a groan. Judith brought the knife up again and tried to control her breathing. The sound seemed close. Straight ahead. She manoeuvred around the body and took a step forward. *Don't get closer, run*, her mind reeled. The two men had killed at least once that she knew of, there was nothing to stop them doing it again. Every nerve in her body jangled as she took another step.

With her attention off the body, she began to notice other things. A long blue pole and a small grey pack lay a few metres ahead. She hesitated and walked forward, straining her ears for any sound. Over the rhythmic beat of the rain and the rustling of the wind, she thought she caught a gurgling sound. It could be a trap. Or, it might be Harper trying to call for help. Her mind leapt from one possibility to another.

Harper could be close by needing help, she had no choice but to push on and find her. Even if it meant risking her own skin. *She'd do it for me*. The thought gave her the strength she needed to stride forward. Within seconds she'd moved up the slope and spotted the mound of dirt. Confused at first, she simply came to a stop and stared.

Judith took in the heap on the far side of what looked like a trench. She heard scraping coming from below and leaned forward. Her heart jumped before she recognised what she saw. Harper lay on her back in the trench. Her eyes closed, blood covering her lips and chin. There was another body nearby, but all Judith could focus on was the still form of the woman she loved.

Judith's legs quivered as she moved forward. The soft dirt shifted under her feet sending her sliding into the trench on her ass. The knife jolted out of her hand. When she came to a stop, her legs touched Harper's.

"Harper?" Judith scrambled forward on her hands and knees.

Harper's clothes were dirty and torn. Her legs, covered in cuts and scratches splayed lifelessly. Judith leaned over her and listened. The pounding of her own heart blocked out all other sound. *She has to be alive.* The familiar ache of loss grew like a lump in her chest.

Judith reached down and touched Harper's face. Her skin felt chilled. "Harper?" She choked out the name.

Time seemed suspended. Judith held her breath and watched her girlfriend's face for signs of life. Harper's eyes moved under their lids and then snapped open. Her legs drew up and then pushed back down as if trying to gain purchase on the wet dirt.

Judith let out a gasp of relief and put her hand on Harper's cheek. She turned her face so they were looking at each other. For an instant, there was only blind panic in the woman's eyes. Seeing her this way, frail and terrorised, made Judith catch her breath. The men who'd done this would pay, she promised herself she'd see to it.

"Jude?" Harper whispered her name around a bubble of blood. "Oh, Jude." Her face crumpled and her shoulders shook.

"It's okay now," Judith leaned down and kissed her on the forehead. "I found you. I won't let them hurt you anymore." As the words tumbled out, Judith realised the truth of them. Above everything else, including her own safety, she had to protect Harper.

"How badly are you hurt?" She wanted to ask other questions, find out what they'd done to her, but now wasn't the time. Getting away from the open pit and somewhere safe had to be her priority.

"I … I don't know." Harper shook her head and coughed. A dribble of pink frothy blood formed at the corner of her mouth.

"It's okay, sweetheart." Judith trailed her fingers across Harper's forehead, brushing the wet tangle of hair away from her face.

She leaned back on her heels and stripped off the hoodie. It was almost wet through, but at least it might offer some comfort. She draped the jacket over Harper's chest and arms. When her hand touched Harper's right arm, she let out a cry of pain.

"Is your arm hurt?" Judith asked.

"Yeah." Harper gave a nod and her whole face seemed to tremble.

"It's okay, sweetheart. I'll be careful." Judith used the torn edge of her shirt to wipe the blood from her girlfriend's mouth.

"He… is he dead?" Harper's words were choked and halting as if she were having trouble breathing.

Judith frowned and then looked over at the other body. The figure of a man lay about a metre and half away. Even prone and on his side, Judith could see his imposing size. She didn't need to ask if he were the one responsible for killing the old man. There was a hulking, menacing aura surrounding him.

"I'll check."

"No." Harper's left hand shot up and grabbed Judith's shirt. She moaned and her arm dropped back over her body. "Don't go near him … He'll hurt you." Harper's eyes were wide and glassy with pain and fear.

"It's alright. I'll be careful…"

"No." Harper coughed. "No. Run. Before he gets up." Harper tried to lift her head. Her eyelids fluttered and she stopped talking.

Judith leaned in and listened. She could hear Harper breathing, a wheezy gasping sound that sent a jolt of panic through Judith's body. She was alive, but in desperate need of medical help. Judith looked around at the vast wilderness and the body nearby. *If only it were that easy*.

She pulled the hoodie up to Harper's chin then crawled around looking for her knife. She had no intention of approaching the man without a weapon in her hand. After a few minutes of running her fingers through wet dirt, she hit something solid. She brushed the dirt away, relieved to see the handle of the penknife. It wasn't much when compared to the hulking figure laying nearby. *It's something*, she told herself and stood up.

The rain petered out. Judith used her free hand to push the wet hair back off her face. She stepped around Harper and approached the man. He was dressed in black pants, his wide shoulder's strained against the fabric of his white vest. Judith held the knife in front of her ready in case he moved. A shaggy mass of dark hair covered the back of his head. She swallowed and bent over him.

His hair looked wet. At first Judith thought from the rain, but on closer inspection, she could see his hair was coated with something thicker. A dip in the back of his skull accompanied a gash running down his neck. Judith glanced over her shoulder. Had Harper caved the man's skull in? *I hope so*, she thought, surprised by her own coldness. She side-stepped the man's head so she could get a look at his face. It was pressed into the dirt with only the left side visible. Judith crouched in front of him with the knife pointed at his neck. If he moved, she'd stab him.

His eye hung open, bulging forward at an unnatural angle. His mouth slack and crusted with dirt. She felt no pity for him, only disgust. Yesterday, she'd have argued that no one deserved to be killed for their crimes. But she'd seen what he'd done to Harper and the old man. If Harper had indeed bashed his skull in, it was what he deserved. *If that makes me a hypocrite, so be it*, she thought with little emotion.

The dropping eyelid blinked. Judith yelped and toppled back onto her ass. His mouth moved, dragging dirt along his lower lip. She held the knife out with a trembling hand. *How is he moving with the back of his head collapsed?* She watched in horror as the eye moved and fixed on her. She knew she should leap forward and stab him before he had the chance to get up. *He can't get up, his head is mush*, her inner voice reminded her.

Judith waited, torn by indecision. She'd felt nothing but relief when she thought he was dead. Maybe even pleasure thinking he'd got what he deserved, yet with the chance to finish him off herself, she'd become frozen, unable to act.

"You!" He spoke with the slushy drawl of a stroke victim.

Judith moved to her left and the bulging eye followed. "I'll kill you," he spluttered. The fingers on his left hand jerked.

Judith jolted back and the man made a wet snuffling sound. She had to act. There was no telling if he might be able to move or hurt them. The shape of his head and the impaired speech made her think he was beyond being a threat. *You thought he was dead a minute ago and you were wrong about that.* Judith chewed on her bottom lip trying to think. A difficult task with the bulging eye glued to her every movement.

It would be best to kill him. Finish him off and then be sure they were safe. Judith looked down at the small knife. Could she do it? Could she plunge the knife into a man's neck in cold blood? A crisp wind blew through the trench. Judith shivered. The man made another snuffling sound and she realised he was laughing at her. The thought of him still enjoying watching someone suffer turned her stomach.

She jumped to her feet and made her way back to Harper, her eyes open and filled with tears. "He's alive," Judith couldn't lie to her even to spare her the worry of knowing a killer was still breathing and only metres away.

"There's a phone," Harper whispered. "It's William's." She spoke haltingly as if struggling to draw enough breath to speak. "Call for help."

Judith nodded. If she could find a phone and call for help, she might be able to get Harper and the others out by nightfall. She guessed William was the old man. Fleetingly she wondered how Harper came to know his name, but didn't waste time asking. She remembered the small pack near the dead man's body. That would be the best place to start looking. The only problem was the other man. She couldn't leave Harper with him.

Judith ran her hand over her mouth. All sorts of possibilities flooded her imagination. Not the least of them, the killer getting to his feet and reaching Harper while Judith was off looking for a phone. She let her gaze fall on the killer. He remained unmoving, but that didn't mean he wouldn't get to his feet the minute she left the trench. She noticed he wore some sort of black nylon utility belt. It gave her an idea.

She left Harper and went back to the injured killer. The hardest part of the plan would be touching him. As much as the thought of putting her hands on him made her skin crawl, Judith had no choice. She knelt down at his back and reached around his waist. She could feel his stomach rising and falling under her hand. He gave a grunt and muttered something incoherent. She found his belt buckle and began working it loose. It quickly became obvious that freeing the belt would be a two-handed job. Judith cursed under her breath and made her way around his body.

His eye, still open, watched her. The glassy orb moved over her body. To get both hands on his belt, she had to kneel in front of him. She could smell sweat and something acrid. She held her breath and worked the buckle as quickly as her cold fingers would allow.

"You'll die." It came out as a slushy breath but there was no mistaking the anger.

"Shut up," Judith snapped and tugged the belt free of his pants.

With the strap in her hands, she moved to get up, then noticed a rectangular bulge in his front left pocket. Her heart jumped in her chest. She reached her hand into the pocket trying to ignore the heat of his legs. Her fingers found the metallic object. As she slid the phone out, he started making the snuffling noise again.

Judith looked up and gasped. One side of his upper lip curled revealing a row of small white teeth. He was smiling at her. She wanted to pull away, close her eyes and try to block the image of his staring eye and pink gums from her mind. Instead she forced herself to hold his gaze.

"Laugh it up freak," she said with all the contempt she could muster. His lip dropped, but the glassy brown eye didn't waver.

Judith positioned herself behind him so that she could tie his wrists behind his back with the belt. Before she started, she checked the phone. It was turned off. She depressed the button and held her breath. It seemed like minutes before the icon appeared and the phone turned on.

"Harper, I've got the phone," she called over her shoulder. Without waiting for an answer, she punched in triple zero and waited. A lump formed in her throat and her heart fluttered. The call connected and a woman asking if she needed fire, police or ambulance.

"I... I need help... Ambulance." She hesitated. "Police too."

"Redirecting your call." The voice sounded disconnected and unemotional.

Within seconds, a female voice clicked on the line and asked her about the nature of the emergency. The words tumbled out so quickly, the woman had to stop her twice and ask her to repeat herself.

"I'm sending police and medical help," the woman said. "Are you in any immediate danger?"

Judith hesitated and glanced at the man's back. Lucas said there were two of them. Maybe the other man was nearby. "Yes." Judith let out a shaky breath. "We're in danger. I don't know where my sister is. She fell and hurt her head."

"Stay on the line." The woman sounded calm, there was kindness in her voice. "Someone will be there soon."

"There's not much charge left in the battery. I don't know how much longer it'll last." Judith felt a finger of panic uncurl in her stomach.

"I have your location, if the phone dies just stay put and wait."

"Yes." Judith nodded even though the woman couldn't see her.

She put the phone on the ground so she'd have her hands free. They weren't in the clear yet. She reached over the man and grabbed his wrist. His skin felt sticky. She pulled his arm behind his back. The other arm was under him. She'd have to roll him forward slightly to get at it.

"Judith are you still there?" The operator's voice sounded loud and urgent.

"Yes," Judith answered through gritted teeth and pushed the man forward. His body felt like a dead weight, but she could hear him making noises and trying to speak.

"Police and medical have been notified, they're on their way."

"Okay." Judith managed to grab hold of his right arm and drag it behind his back. Now the man lay half on his stomach. She wondered briefly if he would be able to breathe, but quickly decided she didn't care.

She fastened the nylon belt around his thick hairy wrists and drew it as tight as possible. Then used the excess to wind around the gap between his hands. When she finished, she gave the belt a tug. It felt secure.

Judith picked up the phone and moved back to Harper's side. The sky, heavy with cloud cover, looked menacing. She checked the time on the phone, 4:20 p.m. The thought of being in the trench with the killer at nightfall made her neck crawl with gooseflesh. *All we have to do now is wait*, she thought.

* * *

"Harper?" It had been ten minutes since she'd called triple zero. "Harper," Judith whispered and touched her girlfriend's face. "I called the police. They're coming. We'll be okay now." Judith tried for a smile.

Harper's eyes fluttered open. "There's two of them." Her voice sounded raspy, as if the words caught in her throat.

"I know, sweetheart. Lucas told me. Now…"

"Lucas is one of them."

Chapter Twenty-Four

Milly wrenched her shoulders free and tried to stand. Lucas grabbed the front of her shirt and pulled her back down. Her eyes moved back to the tattoo on his chest. *Drew 2006* in black cursive above his heart. *It can't be. How could he possibly know Drew?*

"He was my brother," he said, as if answering her unspoken question.

Milly let out a moan. Things fell into place. The feeling of anxiety approaching the cliffs – not because she was with Judith again, but because Lucas's voice, so like Drew's, triggered her memory. Watching Lucas drink from the water bottle, the way his throat moved – in that moment, she'd felt old memories stirring. Time and again her mind had been trying to warn her but she'd been too anxious and worried to put the pieces together.

"You and your sister killed him," his voice shook. He pulled her close, until his face filled her vision. "You took him away from us and then went on with your lives."

Milly could feel his breath against her face. He still held the front of her shirt, the fabric bunched in his fist. She tried to think of something to say that wouldn't fuel his anger. "It was an accident. We never meant…"

"I *hear*d you. You told your sister you pushed him." He laughed. A dry humourless sound that made her stomach clench. "All these years, I knew you'd both had a hand in killing him, but I guess I blamed her more than you." He gave her a shake to emphasise his words. Milly felt her teeth clang together and the pain in her head exploded. "I almost felt sorry for you yesterday."

"Lucas, please." She grabbed at his wrist. "I never meant to hurt him. It's the truth."

"Your truth is lies," he roared into her face, spraying her with spittle and hot breath. "My mother killed herself six months later and they put me and my little brother in foster care." His eyes filled with tears and a purple vein pulsed on his temple.

Milly slumped in his grasp. She deserved his hate *and* anger. A small part of her had always known she'd have to pay for what she'd done. Maybe that's why she'd failed at every relationship she'd ever had, because a part of her knew she didn't deserve happiness.

"You're right," she managed around sobs.

Lucas's mouth dropped open and he released his grip on her shirt. Milly tumbled back onto her butt. "There's nothing I can say to make it right. I … I killed him."

Lucas stood. He towered over her, his fists clenched at his sides. Milly waited for the blows to rain down. *Maybe it's better this way. At least the pain and grief will end and I'll finally have some peace.* Yet even as she tried to reconcile herself to what was about to happen, a small stubborn part of her didn't want to die. The buzzing in her ears kicked in again and she clamped her hand to the side of her head.

Lucas stepped back and his shoulders slumped. "They put me and Archie with a couple who lived in Midland." Milly tried to listen and keep track of what he was saying but a static, fuzzy line of light blurred her eyes and her head felt as if it were vibrating. "The husband, Allan, he seemed okay at first, but then he started messing around with Archie." He caught his breath.

"I'm sorry," she couldn't think of anything else to say.

Lucas bent and lifted the leg of his black pants. A knife in a black nylon sheaf was strapped to his shin. He pulled the knife free, its long blade picked up the light. Milly winced and shrank back.

"Stand up," his voice sounded flat, the tremor of minutes ago vanished. It was as if he'd made up his mind and all the emotion had been swept away.

"Please," Milly spluttered. Her nose ran and tears joined the fuzzy light in her eyes. "I'm sorry for what's happened to you, but you don't have to do this."

"Get up." He took a step towards her.

"Okay." Milly held her hand over her head as if it could shield her from the huge blade. "Okay, I'm getting up." She found her feet and stumbled to her knees. A shaft of agony spliced through her head. For a second, she thought Lucas had stabbed her, but then her vision cleared enough for her to see him still standing a couple of metres away.

"Get to your feet! Don't make me say it again."

She climbed to her feet on sandbag legs. Milly swiped a hand across her nose and her arm came away bloody. She thought of running, but the thought was only brief and fleeting. It seemed all strength had drained from her body. She faced Lucas, swaying slightly to keep her balance.

"You and your sister took everything away from us. Archie was always a messed-up kid, but Drew knew how to handle him. He loved Drew." The cords in his neck bulged. "We all loved Drew." He pointed the knife at her. "You took him away from us!" His voice rose to an angry roar. He rushed forward.

Milly didn't have time to react. She took an awkward backward step, then he was on her. She gasped expecting the pain of the blade, instead he grabbed her shoulders and lifted her off her feet. His fingers sent ribbons of pain down her arms. She felt herself being swept backwards then crashing into something solid and the back of her head crunched against what she guessed was a tree.

Milly groaned. The pain in her head sent shivers through the length of her body. Lucas held her there, her feet barely scraping the ground.

"I've waited years for this," he drew his lips back in a grimace. "This is for Drew." He dropped her to her feet and held her around the throat. Knife drawn back, prepared to strike.

"Just don't hurt my sister." Milly managed to get the words out around the pressure on her throat. Tears ran down her cheeks mixing with blood and mucus.

He hesitated, "What did you say?" His face little more than a blur.

"Do it, but don't hurt Judith. None of it's her fault."

His fingers loosened and then released. Milly gasped in air. The lights in her eyes grew brighter until she could see nothing but red and gold. It was beautiful. Her legs folded under her and she toppled to the side.

Chapter Twenty-Five

"You mean Lucas is part of this?" Judith waved her arm towards the killer.

Harper grimaced and nodded. Her skin looked grey as if the life had been drained from her body. Judith leaned over her and put her face on Harper's shoulder. Her ear brushed against her girlfriend's neck. Her skin felt chilled. *What now?* Her mind raced. She'd left her sister with a killer. He could be doing anything to Milly right now. Judith pulled her head back.

"I... I left Milly with him." Judith felt tears building up. She wiped at her nose. She could hardly believe what she was about to say. She'd fought so hard to find Harper and now she was thinking of leaving her. "I have to go and help her." She searched Harper's eyes for any trace of hurt or disapproval.

"Help her." Harper's lips were stained with blood.

Judith kissed her cheeks and forehead. She wished she could tear herself in two so that she didn't have to leave Harper alone again. She cupped her girlfriend's face in her hands. She'd been through so much; Judith wanted to stay with her and cradle her head until the medics arrived, but how could she turn her back on her sister?

Milly's face flashed in her mind: cheeks stained with dirt, eyes raw and red rimmed. She'd begged Judith not to leave. *We'll talk when this is over*, that was the last thing she said before walking away and leaving her sister with a killer. A crow screeched from a nearby tree. Soon others joined it until the branches were filled with the evil-looking black birds. *A murder of crows.* Judith shivered.

There was no telling how long it would take the police and medics to arrive, by then Milly could be dead. If she acted now, there might be time to save her. She couldn't sit and ignore the chance to save her sister's life. *Not when we've just found each other again.* Judith forced the tears back. She wouldn't waste time crying, she had too much to do. She couldn't afford to let her emotions overtake her.

"I'll be back," she said to Harper and scampered out of the pit.

Judith didn't want to look at the old man again so she gave him a wide berth. The small pack was where it had been when she first found the body. She crouched down over it, keeping her back to the old man's body. *William.* Harper called him William. Inside, she found a light weight jacket and a half empty bottle of water. Judith pulled out the jacket and took a gulp of the water. She thought about giving some to Harper, but wondered if she ought to wait until the medics assessed her injuries.

At the bottom of the pack she spotted a packet of crackers. Judith's stomach groaned. The last thing she'd eaten was an energy bar, hours before. She tore the bag open and stuffed a few crackers in her mouth before washing them down with a swig of water. The crackers were dry and tasteless, but it felt wonderful to have something in her empty stomach.

Back in the pit, Judith pulled the damp hoodie off Harper's upper body and replaced it with the dry jacket. She folded the hoodie and slipped it under Harper's head. "Better?"

Harper gave a nod. "Be … careful." Harper's eyes were wet with tears. Her mouth trembled. Seeing her this way brought a lump to Judith's throat.

She glanced over at the man laying with his hands bound. He'd done this to Harper. The urge to run over and kick him in the back swept through her. She watched his back and shoulders. His body looked slack, she hoped he was dead. About to turn away, Judith noticed something black against his back. It stuck up from under his pants and bulged out the back of his vest. She wondered why she didn't notice it earlier. Probably because she'd been too distracted by his caved in skull and bulging eye.

She left Harper and crouched behind the man's back. His shirt had come untucked and caked in dirt. The thought of touching him again set her teeth on edge. She pulled the edge of his shirt with the tips of her fingers and lifted it up.

"Jesus," Judith gasped out the word. A large black nylon sheaf was strapped to his back. In it, a hunting knife with a maroon handle.

She pulled the blade from the sheaf and held it up. It felt fairly weighty for a knife. The blade was large with a slight curve; it looked like something used to kill big game. *Is that what we are to him?* Judith noticed there were dark stains around the base and handle. *William's blood?* The idea of holding a knife used to kill someone made her stomach lurch. She took a deep breath and fought back the urge to vomit. She wanted to drop it, but if she were going looking for her sister, she might need more than a penknife.

She leaned over his body, her fingers brushing against the skin on his belly and coming into contact with a patch of coarse damp hair. Judith cringed and pulled her hand away, deciding she would make do without the sheaf. She cut a section off the back of the man's white vest. The blade sliced through the fabric so easily that Judith grimaced. The pale skin of the base of his spine lay exposed. Judith wondered what it would feel like if she drove the hunting knife into that patch of skin. *It might be safer to just kill him.* The thought frightened and appealed to her at the same time. She imagined herself grabbing his shoulder with one hand and driving in the blade with the other. He'd probably scream and thrash. She realised the urge to kill him had nothing to do with safety, she wanted to do it. He deserved it.

"What are you doing?" The slushy voice startled her.

"Shut the fuck up," Judith snapped. She wrapped the fabric around the knife then slid it into her back pocket. Hopefully the wrapping would stop the knife shifting and slicing into her butt.

Snuffling laughter came from the heap on the ground. Judith stood up and stepped around him so she could look into the bulging glassy eye. She opened her mouth to tell him the police were on their way when he spoke again.

"Shut the fuck up. That's what I said …" He drew in a wet breath. "To your mother just before I pushed her down the stairs." His eye blinked.

Judith's mouth dropped open. It felt like the air had been sucked out of her lungs. She wanted to scream and call him a liar, but her thoughts wouldn't connect with her voice. How could it be? Had he killed her mother? Was he lying? But how did he know her mother fell down the stairs? Her mother had been something of a celebrity, but only to readers dedicated to her romance novels. Judith supposed this mad man could have looked her up, but the public were told she'd fallen while home alone. No other details were given.

He made that snuffling sound again. It reminded Judith of the noise a pig makes when it eats. He was laughing at her. She had the urge to pull the knife out of her pocket and stab him. She reached around the back of her shorts and gripped the handle. It felt slick and cold in her hand. She was about to slide it out when another more horrifying thought occurred to her.

If Lucas was with this man *and* they were involved in her mother's death, then all that had happened wasn't just random or opportunistic. The two of them had to have planned this. Judith let go of the knife and tried to block out the wet snuffling sounds. *How could I be so stupid?* Of course they'd planned it. Lucas had been manipulating them all along. It was his idea to bring Milly to the National Park. His idea to abseil. She tried to remember the first time that the notion of not just getting Milly alone but frightening her came into play. Her heart fluttered at the memory; they'd climbed a rock face in some bushland near Kalamunda. Harper said something about losing her footing and how scary it felt. The moment so unimportant at the time, became the spike on which everything hung. Lucas nodding his head, leaning back on his muscular arms agreeing with everything they said. Judith caught her breath.

She could almost hear his voice, "That's why abseiling is such a good idea." Then, like a sound bite from a movie clip. "Nothing bonds people like a near death experience."

"You bastard." The words slipped off her lips. If she hadn't been so focused on Milly and forcing her to admit the truth, she'd have seen it sooner. She'd been hell-bent, not only on getting Milly where she wanted her, but on punishing her.

Judith clamped her hand over her mouth. *Was it ever about the truth or did I just want to make her suffer for letting me take all the blame?* Her tunnel vision had ultimately put them all in danger. She'd let Lucas get the three of them out here alone. Then he'd arranged for his buddy to join him for some sick fun in the bush. It made perfect sense, but didn't explain why they would have hurt her mother.

Judith stooped down. "You're a liar." Her voice came out as little more than a strangled whisper.

"Am I?" he asked in that mushy voice she'd come to loathe.

Being close to him made her cringe. The thought of him in her mother's house, his face the last thing she might have seen; it was almost too much.

"Why?" she asked, hating even giving him the satisfaction of her curiosity. But as much as he made her skin crawl, she had to know the truth.

"When my brother gets here, you're gonna wish you ran away as fast as your sweet legs could carry you."

His brother. So this animal was Lucas's brother. That didn't explain why they were doing this. Why they'd hurt Harper, killed William and terrorised Judith and Milly. Then there was her mother, what possible reason could they have for killing her? Judith longed to bombard the man with questions, but he seemed to enjoy playing with her. She felt certain he wouldn't give her any real answers and she didn't have time to waste.

"I've called the police." Judith tried to keep her voice unemotional. "They'll be here soon, if you live that long."

"Your bitch won't last another ten minutes." He took a slurpy breath. His one staring eye blinked with excitement.

Judith pulled back. Even in the chilly afternoon air, her face felt hot. Hot with anger and hurt. She thought of saying something smart back but time was short and nothing she said would penetrate his madness.

She made her way back to Harper. The phone lay on the ground beside her. Judith checked it and found it dead. "Damn." To Harper she said, "I'm going now. It won't be long before the medics get here." She kissed Harper's chilly skin. "You hang on. I love you."

Harper managed a half-smile half-grimace. "Be careful. I love you too."

Chapter Twenty-Six

Harper listened to Judith's boots scuffing the earth as she climbed out of the pit. She could feel the tears streaming down the side of her face leaving icy trails on her skin. Her body felt chilled as if the cold ground beneath her had seeped through her skin and touched her bones.

Part of her felt high with elation. Judith was alive and help was on its way. But another part of her felt numb with fear. What would Lucas do to Judith? What had he already done to Milly? Harper remembered the moment when Milly fell while climbing down the cliff. Even then there'd been something suspicious about the accident. She'd felt it in her bones. God how she wished she'd spoken up then, done something. In her mind she could see the moment as clear as if it were happening all over again.

Standing behind Lucas, Harper could see him working the ropes. He looked relaxed, his voice confident. Harper knew the plan, to wait until Milly was a metre or so off the ground and then let her drop. She didn't like the idea, but she'd let Judith talk her into it. *You could have just said no*, she reminded herself. But she hadn't said *no*. She'd agreed to go along with Judith's plan.

She'd taken a step closer to Lucas, trying to watch Milly's descent. She took her eyes off Lucas's hands and leaned over to get a better view. Suddenly Milly dropped. Her mouth formed a shocked circle, her eyes wide and panicked. Then the smack as she hit the ground. Harper heard herself scream, a raw pained noise.

"Milly?" Both Judith and Harper had called her name.

Harper, from her vantage point above could see the top of Judith's hat as she bent over her sister. "Milly? Milly, please." The pain in Judith's voice cut Harper like a knife.

"Is she okay?" Lucas sounded concerned, but there was no panic in his voice.

Judith looked up. "I don't know. I don't know. She's breathing but she's out cold. What should I do?"

"Put her in the coma position," Harper remembered doing a first aid course a few years earlier as part of her teacher training.

"No. Don't move her." Lucas sounded calm, the voice of reason. "Unclip the harness, but don't try and move her. She might have spinal damage."

"Oh God!" Judith wailed and began unclipping the clasps from her sister's body.

It struck Harper as strange that he wanted the harness unclipped. What difference did it make? But the moment Judith had the straps off Milly's body, Lucas pulled the rig up and stuffed it in his bag. *Why are we wasting time with all this?* Before she could voice her thoughts, Lucas started giving orders.

"You stay with her and we'll go for help," he'd called down the cliff.

Judith stumbled to her feet and pulled her hat off. "Harper?" She looked up with terrified eyes. Harper knew she was waiting for her to tell her what to do.

"I should stay," Harper turned to Lucas. "I can't leave her alone down there."

Lucas finished stowing his climbing gear and picked up his pack. "There's no way down that won't take hours. If we pick up the pace and jog, we'll be near the trail in forty minutes." He swung the pack over his shoulder and picked up Judith's red nylon bag. "We should be able to get a signal then and call for help."

Harper could feel a line of sweat gathering on the back of her neck. The afternoon sun sat high in the sky and the air felt heavy. "No. I'll stay up here and wait for the medics to arrive."

Lucas grabbed her arm and pulled her back from the edge. His fingers dug into her skin. For a second, Harper could have sworn she'd seen something cruel in his features. But it disappeared just as quickly, leaving her wondering if what she'd really seen was panic.

"Listen," he lowered his voice. "We need to get Milly help right away. If I go alone and fall or get bitten by a snake, she'll die before you two realise no one's coming." Harper gasped. "It has to be the two of us. It's the only safe option."

* * *

Fifteen minutes later, Harper jogged behind Lucas as they headed back to the trail. The only sounds came from the chatter of cockatoos in the trees as they cracked open seed pods, and the thump of their boots on the dirt. Her mind kept coming back to the moment Milly fell. Dropping her was part of the plan, but did he do it from a greater height on purpose? She wondered why they weren't trying the phone to see if they could get a signal.

Harper stopped moving and dropped her pack on the ground. Her bag contained two mobile phones, her own and Milly's. Now that the initial shock of seeing her friend fall had begun to subside, Harper's brain seemed to be functioning clearly. She'd taken Milly's phone while pretending to help close her pack. It had been part of the plan. Judith didn't want Milly calling for help the minute she thought they were stranded. *How could I have run off and left them without a phone?* Once the plan had gone haywire, the logical thing would've been to give Judith the phone while Harper and Lucas went for help. *Then why didn't you?* Harper asked herself. The answer was simple. Lucas had rushed her away while she was still reeling from the accident. *Was it an accident?*

"What are you doing?" Lucas's voice broke through her reverie.

Harper looked up. The sun was behind him. Raising her hand to shield her eyes, she tried to squint away the glare. She could make out his shape, large and dark, haloed by glaring sunlight.

"I'm going to see if I can get a signal." Harper couldn't make out his features, but there was something menacing in his stance. In that moment, she became acutely aware of being alone with this man miles from anywhere.

"You're wasting time. We need to keep moving." His voice sounded tight, almost angry.

Harper reminded herself that he was probably behaving strangely because of the accident. After all, he'd dropped Milly. The shock and guilt of that would be enough to shake anyone up. Even so, she thought it best to not aggravate the situation. "Yes. You're right," she tried to keep her tone casual. "I'll just check if I've got a signal and then we'll go."

A flash of black darted out of the glare. Lucas snatched the pack out of her hands. "Stop fucking about," he growled. His hand slid under her arm and wrenched her to her feet.

"What?" Harper stuttered.

"Move." Lucas pushed her forward.

Harper stumbled and nearly lost her footing on the uneven ground. She tried to turn around, but Lucas's large hand slapped the base of her back and shoved her forward. This time she *did* lose her balance. Her boots skidded on a patch of loose stones. She tried to correct her balance and nose-dived into the dirt with a tooth-jarring thud.

Too shocked and breathless to speak, Harper flopped over onto her back. Her first reaction, outrage. *He actually pushed me*, her mind screamed. Then more sinister thoughts overtook all other feelings and she began to realise she might be in danger. Lucas loomed over her. There was no trace of the shy, almost lost, young man she'd befriended at the gym. Her instincts told her to run but with him so close, she doubted she'd get far before he grabbed her.

"Get up and move!" The last word turned into a bellow.

Harper flinched and scrambled to her feet. She wanted to argue, but the clamp of his hand on her shoulder silenced her. Whatever Lucas had in mind, she had no choice but to go along with it, at least for now.

After ten minutes of hiking over uneven ground, with Lucas squeezing her shoulder, Harper snapped. She dipped her right shoulder and sidestepped to the left. Lucas, caught by surprise, lost his grip. Seizing the opportunity, Harper turned and ran. Still heading for the trail, she found herself fighting against shrubs and shaggy trees. Her pack bounced against her shoulders. Still moving forward, she shrugged the straps off her shoulders and let the pack drop behind her.

Lucas's footfalls thumped the earth, the sound competing with the hammering of her heart. She rounded a jagged crop of granite and collided with a solid mass. The impact smashed the air out of her lungs and sent her sprawling onto her back. Harper had hit the ground, her tail bone striking something raised and blunt.

Lucas had gotten in front of her. *How could that be?* Her panicked mind tried to make sense of what she was seeing. *No, not Lucas*, but someone who looked very similar; only this guy was bigger, his face scarred with deep pock marks.

"Where are *you* going?" He grinned, exposing unusually small teeth. Harper tried to crab-walk backwards. "No you don't." He reached out a muscular arm and grabbed the front of her shirt.

Harper batted his hand and kicked out with her feet. He ignored her attempts and pulled her up. Wrapping his arm around her waist, he spun her until he had her back to him and then pulled her close and pressed himself against her. A sour musky smell invaded her nostrils.

"I've got her," he called as Lucas rounded the rocks.

Lucas nodded, his face solemn. He sauntered towards them breathing heavily. *Obviously his physique comes from lifting weights, but his aerobic fitness is pathetic.* The thought didn't give Harper any satisfaction, instead a finger of ice travelled up her spine. She was at their mercy. She didn't want to give either of them the pleasure of seeing her cry, but tears blurred her eyes and she was powerless to stop them.

If Lucas noticed her crying, he made no comment. He stood a few metres ahead of them and regarded her. When he spoke, it was to the man behind her. "You been waiting long?"

The man holding her, buried his face in the back of her neck and sniffed. "Yeah, but it's okay. I like it here." When he spoke, his hot breath sprayed the back of her neck. Harper hunched her shoulders and pulled her head forward.

"Lucas, why are you doing this? Please just let me go." Harper hated the tremble in her voice. "I won't say anything to anyone."

"My name's not Lucas. It's Martin. Martin Crowell." He jerked his chin up. "That's my brother Archie."

Harper sucked in air as if jolted by an electric shock. Crowell was Drew's last name. That meant these two men holding her captive were his family? How could she have been so blind? The resemblance was there as clear as day. Only it had been ten years since she last saw Drew. Over time his face had blurred in her memory. Now, looking into Lucas's eyes, she could see the truth. *No, not Lucas,* she reminded herself. *Martin.* A ghost from the past. Harper's legs quivered.

"So this is about revenge?" she asked, trying to keep the tremble from her voice.

"Those two." He jerked his thumb over his shoulder. "They didn't just kill our brother, they destroyed our family. When I saw you at the gym, I recognised you straight away. Archie and me were at the inquest with our mother. You probably didn't even notice us." He gave a smile that reminded her of lightening flashing. "You were too busy supporting your friends to notice two kids who'd just lost their brother."

"Luc…" she stopped herself. "Martin, nobody meant to hurt Drew. What happened …" She searched for an explanation. Words that would show these men how sorry she was, but apologies seemed empty. "I liked Drew," she said. "He was a good guy."

Martin flinched. Whatever he'd been expecting her to say, that wasn't it. Something flickered across his face. It might have been regret, but the look vanished. Sensing she'd found a weak spot, Harper pushed on. "Drew wouldn't want this. He wouldn't want his brothers hurting people."

"You barely knew him!" he snapped. "You don't know anything."

"I know he was a good guy." She searched for the words. "Kind and genuine. He'd hate what you're doing."

Martin stepped closer, his face red with emotion. Regret or anger, Harper couldn't tell. "I don't expect someone like you to get it. We have to do this." He looked at the man holding her. "My brothers deserve payback. Payback for what happened to Drew *and* Archie."

Archie gave a grunt of agreement.

"It's the only way." Martin continued. "Once this is over, things can be better again. Archie and me are leaving Western Australia. Going to start a new life."

"So now what?" She took a shaky breath. "You and your brother are going kill me?"

"Not straight away," the one holding her, Archie, whispered close to her ear. His arms, enfolding her waist squeezed and she felt herself being lifted off the ground.

It was the chance she'd been waiting for. *You won't get another*, she told herself and leaned back against Archie. She swung her legs upwards, the side of her boot caught Martin under the right side of his forehead with a hollow thud. He staggered left.

"Hey!" Archie sounded more surprised than angry.

Before he had time to react, Harper drew her knees up and pumped them out into Martin's chest. Pushing off his ribs like a swimmer pushing off the side of the pool. Martin had lost his balance and hit the ground. At the same time, Archie stumbled backwards. Harper felt Archie falter and threw herself back with enough force to topple both of them over.

Archie smacked the ground and let out an "Oomph." Harper landed on top of him. He let go of her waist to steady himself. She saw her chance and took off like a bull out of a gate. Head down, arms pumping she headed right, towards the trees with the cold wind slapping her face. Behind her she heard Archie bellow something and then rush after her.

* * *

"Harper?"

She opened her eyes. Above her the sky hung low with dark clouds backlit by streaks of orange. She moved the fingers on her right hand, scraping the wet dirt. She was still in the pit. How long had it been since Judith left? She had no idea but the fading light told her evening approached.

She sniffed and the odour of damp earth filled her nose. She tried to lift her head and a shard of agony pierced her chest. She dropped her head and lay still, panting.

"Harper?"

There it was again. The voice drifted across the pit, high and mocking, but with a wet slurp on the *r*.

He was close by. She could feel his nearness. Judith tied him up, but maybe he'd freed himself somehow. *No*, Aunty Joan's voice spoke up. *He'll never get up again. You bashed his head in.* Harper visualized the rock hitting the back of Archie's head and heard the crack of his skull. A sound that reminded her of the day she'd dropped a honey dew melon when unloading groceries from the boot of her car. The melon hit the concrete and broke open, spilling pinkish orange pulp in a gloopy puddle. Archie's skull had cracked like that melon. Harper swallowed. *Would she ever stop hearing that sound?*

She waited. Listened. Imagining Archie lumbering towards her, head hanging at an unnatural angle, angry eyes bulging, glaring, accusing her of trying to kill him. A sound. Harper yelped.

She closed her eyes. She had no strength left to run or fight. Whatever happened now, she'd have to face alone. The seconds stretched out. She waited. A whirring growl echoed over the pit. Not the sound of a dead man's feet shuffling across the dirt, but a helicopter. Harper opened her mouth to laugh and a sob ripped from between her lips. In the distance a dog barked.

Chapter Twenty-Seven

Judith braced herself against a gum tree and bent forward. She took long even breaths, massaging her left side just above the hip. Her legs itched with the desire to move, but she knew if she didn't work out the stitch, she'd be forced to stop again in less than a minute. Every second wasted could mean the difference between life and death. *No*, she told herself. *I won't accept that. Milly's okay. I just have to get to her in time.*

Her plans didn't stretch as far as what she would do when she found Lucas and her sister. Maybe she wouldn't have to do anything. He didn't make any move to hurt her when she was with Milly. The possibility that Lucas was a coward who could only strike when he got a woman alone crossed her mind. She wondered if without his brother he was powerless to act. *Or getting us one by one is part of their sick game.* Her thoughts shifted back and forth on an endless loop of hope and despair.

The cramp in her side eased and Judith straightened her back. She remembered something Lucas said when he stumbled upon them earlier that day. He mentioned wandering around in the dark, then hearing the screams. It had bothered her all day, but until now it hadn't occurred to her that the screaming started before it got dark. If she'd been thinking clearly, instead of arguing with Milly, she'd have realised he was lying. She only hoped Milly wouldn't pay for her mistakes.

The forest around her lay in shadows with only murky light filtering through the storm clouds. She slid her hand down the tree and pushed off. Heading south seemed the safest course of action. That way, she'd run along the path Milly and Lucas would take if they were heading back to the trail. *He could be leading her deeper into the wilderness*, a voice in her head whispered. No, his brother was near the hiking trail and as far as Lucas knew, so was Judith. He'd head back, she felt sure of it.

Judith jogged through the trees. Branches and sticks grabbed at her arms and clothing. She slapped them away and tripped on the sloping ground, her knees pounding the dirt. Her legs trembled with the strain. She'd been on the move for hours, running on sips of water, crackers, and an energy bar. She didn't know how much more her body could take. She took hold of a fallen log and pushed herself up. Her knees were bloody, the red a stark contrast against her grubby legs. She wondered how Milly was holding up. Had Lucas hurt her? Killed her? She couldn't let her thoughts take her in that direction. She had to believe her sister was alive.

Minutes later, Judith felt the wilderness thin and spaces grow wider. She wandered into an open area where bush grasses reached as high as her knees. Hands on hips, she looked up and sucked in gulps of air. The light was softer, almost murky on the green and yellow waves of the wild grass. The urge to lay down in the coolness of the damp clearing and close her eyes almost overwhelmed her. Her knees began to fold of their own accord. Judith covered her face with her hands trying to will her body to keep moving.

On the other side of the clearing lay a small scattering of trees, their limbs twisted and bent from a lifetime of strong westerly winds coming off the Indian Ocean. Branches shimmered and undulated as if moved by an unseen force. Judith frowned and stepped back confused by what she saw. Her hand reached behind her and hovered over the knife. Suddenly the trees shook as a flock of white cockatoos rose out of the foliage and into the dusky sky. Their startled shrieks filled the air as hundreds of powerful wings batted their way east.

The urgency of the birds' screams turned Judith's bones to ice. They seemed to be screaming at her, warning her. She lurched forward and broke into a run. Within a minute, she'd crossed the clearing and entered the trees. The weak light threw shadows and streaks of grey in every direction. Judith halted and strained her eyes against the dimness. When her vision adjusted, she began to make out a shape.

At first her mind registered another fallen log, but a second glance revealed the truth. Milly's right arm lay half-buried in damp leaves, the white skin of her forearm a stark contrast against the brown foliage; her face turned to the sky as if watching something intently. Judith opened her mouth to call to her sister, but the words caught in her throat. Milly's legs, still clad in black track pants, were barely visible on the forest floor. The stillness of her sister's form seemed unnatural.

Judith moved closer and spoke, "Milly?" Her voice sounded small and childish like a frightened child calling her big sister when everyone else was asleep. "Mil?" Judith's shoulders quivered. She flopped down next to her sister, her head bobbing with exhaustion.

Milly's hazel eyes were open, her lashes damp as if she'd been crying. A soggy brown leaf clung to her left cheek. Without thinking, Judith reached out and brushed it away. She pulled her hand back as if it had been slapped. Her sister's skin felt lifeless, like damp clay still soft and malleable, but without warmth or vitality. A smear of blood, dark and dry lined Milly's upper lip.

Judith's heart wavered, missing a beat then righting itself. Instinctively, she put her hand to her chest. *We'll talk when this is over.* Judith's body sagged, she screwed her eyes closed as her sister's pleading face flashed in her mind. *I did this to her.* The guilt hit her like a punch in the chest. *I brought her out here promising a reconciliation. I dangled it in front of her knowing she'd come and then ...* Judith's thoughts faltered. She raised her hands as if pleading with her sister's lifeless form, then dropped then in her own lap.

I knew she'd come if I asked, Judith thought bitterly. *She always came running if she thought I needed her.* Even that night at Blackwell Reach, Milly had been so desperate to save her sister, she'd panicked and pushed Drew off the cliff.

"Oh, Mil." Judith let out a shuddering sob. "Don't go."

She picked up Milly's hand, flinching at the feel of her rapidly cooling skin. The nails were dirty and the skin streaked with grime. Judith stroked the back of her sister's hand. *She was really hurt and I didn't even say anything kind.* Judith pressed her sister's hand against her own forehead and swayed back and forth.

Minutes passed, Judith wasn't sure how long she held Milly's hand, only that the light dimmed. Her throat burned and her face felt raw. Sound began to register – insects chirped and branches rustled. She put Milly's hand down, laying it across her sister's chest. Before standing, she allowed herself one last look at her sister's face. Milly's hazel eyes looked dull, clouded.

Judith pulled her gaze away. Thoughts of Lucas and what he'd done to her sister pushed through the grief. He was a killer. His brother killed William and brutalised Harper, was it any surprise that Lucas was just as dangerous? *He's no better than an animal.* A cold lump formed in her chest. She clenched her teeth and turned away from her big sister's body. She wanted Lucas dead. Whatever warped scenario he was playing out, she intended to put a stop to it.

"You're back," his husky voice startled her. Judith spun around.

A maze of trees and shadows. Everywhere she looked, tall dark shapes. Judith's pulse quickened. She flicked her head left then right, damp hair sticking to her face. Had she heard his voice or imagined him behind her? The evening air carried a chilly wind, stirred the branches and whispered through the forest. She'd left the hoodie folded under Harper's head. In only a denim shirt and shorts, Judith shivered.

"I was going to come looking for you," his voice bounced off the trees, buffeted by the wind. "Did you run into Archie?"

Judith resisted the urge to reach for the knife. When he approached, he wouldn't be expecting her to be armed. She hoped it might give her an advantage. "You're a psycho," Her voice trembled. "You and your brother."

The seconds ticked by. The wind made it difficult to hear his movements. From the corner of her left eye, she thought she caught a shifting. Judith whipped around, breath puffing out in short gasps. Branches and shadows merged together making it impossible to distinguish a human form. A crackle of leaves to her right. Judith jerked around.

For a moment, she saw only trees turned grey by the dying light, then her eyes picked up his shape. Lucas stood maybe eight or nine metres away between a grass tree and a thin gum. His broad frame filled the gap with solid darkness. Judith's heart rate ratcheted up another notch. Her hands were trembling so violently, she wondered if she could even grasp the knife.

"That's funny, Judith," he laughed. The sound set her teeth on edge. "You calling me a psycho. You and your sister killed my brother, but you think I'm a psycho."

Judith shook her head trying to process his words. What did he mean? Archie wasn't dead. She opened her mouth to protest when he raised his head and his face appeared from the shadows. *How did I not see it! His voice, his eyes. Oh God, even the shape of his face. Drew.* He was talking about Drew not Archie. Judith took a step back. It was like seeing a ghost. The ghost of his long dead brother inhabited his face.

Lucas stepped forward, his arms relaxed at his sides. A shaft of light fell across his face and Judith realised why she hadn't recognised him. Mostly because it had been ten years since she'd last seen Drew, but also because Lucas was different in one fundamental way. There was no spark of kindness in his countenance. Drew, at least the Drew she remembered, had a kind, open face. There was something compelling in his voice and features. In comparison, Lucas looked coarse and brutish.

"What happened to Drew was an accident." Judith shuffled back another few centimetres. "We never meant for him to ..." Not sure how to finish, she let her words trail off.

"Die?" Lucas offered. "The accident thing doesn't really work now, does it?"

"It *was* an accident." Judith kept her eyes on him and tried to move to her left.

He side-stepped with her. "I heard Milly. When you two thought I was unconscious." He waved his hand and for the first time, Judith noticed he held a knife. "So don't say it was an accident." His voice took on a cold edge. "Me and Archie, we've heard that for ten years. We didn't believe it then, and…" he stretched out the word, "I don't believe it now. Not when I had it straight from the horse's mouth." He pointed the knife to the left.

Judith couldn't help looking over her shoulder to where her sister lay motionless. The sight of Milly's body brought the horror rushing back. Judith felt a fresh wave of grief threaten to crush her. She tore her gaze away and made herself focus on the man in front of her. His stance now less relaxed and more threatening, Lucas began to close the gap between them. Judith searched for something to say. Anything that would keep him talking and give her time to think.

"Is that why you killed my mother?"

Lucas blinked several times in succession. "It wasn't me, it…" He stopped. His brow wrinkled. "How do you know?"

Judith licked her lips. She had his attention now. Maybe telling him about Archie might take his focus off her. On the other hand, finding out Harper had bashed his brother's skull in might push him over the edge.

"Your brother, Archie, he's the one that killed my mother. Why? Did you tell him to? We killed Drew, so you and your brother kill my mother and my sister." Her voice cracked on the last word. Before he could speak, she continued, "I don't think that's it though. I think your brother is a psychopath who enjoys killing." She put her hands on her hips edging the fingers around her back towards the knife. "Maybe you do too."

Lucas lifted his jaw, she could see the muscles in his neck bunched and straining. "You don't get to judge us." He pointed the knife at her. "You're a killer just like her." He motioned to Milly only this time Judith refused to look where he pointed. "Archie was a mixed-up kid, but Drew was good with him." Even in the dim light, Judith could see Lucas's eyes take on a dreamy look. "Dad left when we were little, but it didn't matter 'cause we had each other. Mum relied on Drew, he was going places and we were going with him." He hesitated, running his free hand through his thick, dark hair. "When he died, Mum couldn't cope. She started drinking again and then one day … One day, she stepped in front of a train."

Judith let out a long breath. She didn't want to hear his story. Listen to his crazy reasoning, but she found herself imagining what it must have been like for the two boys losing their brother and then the only person they had left.

"They put us in a foster home," Lucas's voice hardened. "Allan, that was his name – he started doing things to Archie. He was just a kid, thirteen." He sniffed and swiped at his nose with the back of his hand. The blade caught the light. "When Archie told me, I tried to stop Allan ... He hit me so hard, his fist broke my eye socket."

"Lucas, I'm so sorry." She hadn't meant to speak but the words were out before she could stop herself. Once she'd spoken, Judith realised how much she meant what she said. But her words seemed to only anger him.

"We don't need your pity." He took a step closer. "A couple of years ago, Archie paid Allan a surprise visit. His face creased in a grin that made the hairs on the back of Judith's neck stand up. "Allan won't be messing with any more kids."

"Lucas please."

"My name's not Lucas. It's Martin. Martin Crowell." He chuckled. "The Werd part was Archie's idea. He's always been a clever kid. Werd, Drew backwards. Smart, huh?"

Judith shuffled her feet back, just a fraction. "Do you really think you're helping your brother by letting him kill people? By killing my sister?"

"I didn't kill your sister. You did." His words hit her like a slap in the face.

"No ... You did. I found her there." Judith turned her body and looked to where her sister's body lay sprawled near a tree.

"You told me to let her drop. That was the deal, right?" Judith turned back to Lucas. No, not Lucas, she reminded herself. Martin. "What are you talking about?" Even as she asked, a part of her began to understand. There were no marks on Milly. No stab wounds. No signs of violence.

"The fall killed her. It just took a bit longer than it should have."

Judith moaned. Not wanting to hear anymore. "My guess is, a fractured skull. She must have been in a world of pain by the end. That's down to you." He pointed the knife at her chest.

She shook her head. *Maybe he's lying.* She latched onto the idea but couldn't make herself believe it. Her stomach clenched, acrid liquid filled her mouth. She lurched sideways and let the foul-tasting bile spew out. The mess hit the ground, plopping on fallen leaves and damp earth with a thick dribbling sound.

Her arms were suddenly jerked behind her. Martin pulled her backwards pushing her wrists together until her shoulders burned with the strain. Judith gasped, being yanked backwards. She could hear him grunt with the effort of moving her. Her feet kicked out in front of her skidding through twigs and forest rubble. She tried to keep pace with his movements.

He spun her sideways and the forest and sky swirled around her. The left side of her face collided with something solid. The impact snapped her teeth together and Judith bit the inside of her cheek. Sickly sweet blood filled her mouth.

With her face pressed against the rough bark of a pine tree, Judith struggled to keep her footing. Martin's hands clutched her forearms, pressing them together behind her back.

"I'm not enjoying this, Judith. But the sooner it's over, the sooner Archie and me can move on." He pressed his face against the back of her neck, she could feel his breath on her skin. *Where was his knife?* Her mind worked frantically. He'd used both his hands to swing her around, maybe he'd dropped the knife.

As if hearing her thoughts, Martin let go of her arms. The burning pressure on her shoulders released and Judith whistled out a breath between her teeth. The weight of his hand pressed the flesh between her shoulders, pinning her to the tree. She heard his shirt rustle. Something cold pressed against her right cheek.

"I've called the police," she made her voice flat and unafraid. "They'll be here soon. Don't make things worse for yourself, stop all this now." With her hands free but still behind her, she felt for the knife hidden under her shirt.

Lucas's body twitched and shifted against her. "You're lying. Archie's got the phones."

Now it was Judith's turn to laugh. When her lips parted, she felt blood trickle down her chin. "You and your brother are not as smart as you think." Her fingers worked the fabric of her shirt, flicking it back and out of the way.

"What are you talking about?" His face pressed close to her ear, she guessed he must be crouching behind her.

"You both thought he could take Harper on his own." Judith chuckled spraying blood through her lips. "Last time I saw him, he was in bad shape. Harper really put him out of action." Her fingers closed around the hunk of fabric covering the knife's handle.

"You're a fucking liar!" Martin bellowed into her ear.

Judith winced and swallowed blood. "See for yourself." She twisted her head around so she could see Martin's face. "I cut a piece of his vest off just before I tied him up." Her voice sounded raspy and cruel. She almost didn't recognise it as her own. "He wasn't able to put up a struggle by then."

"What?"

She caught Martin's confused frown in the corner of her eye. He stepped back to see what she was reaching for. The pressure between her shoulders released. Judith slid the knife out of her back pocket and turned her right shoulder so she was almost side on with the middle of his body.

He still crouched behind her, knees bent slightly. His gaze on the torn piece of fabric. She couldn't see his hands but knew he still held his knife ready to strike.

"Where did you…"

Holding her knife at an awkward angle behind her back, Judith lunged out and downwards. The blade landed in the muscle of Martin's thigh. It slid through his flesh with a wet slurp. He screamed and stumbled back clutching at the handle. Judith broke free and ran. Ahead of her a jagged shaft of light fell between the trees. The clearing she'd crossed lay ahead. She knew if she made it into the open, he'd never be able to catch her, not with an injured leg. She broke into a sprint.

Chapter Twenty-Eight

Harper raised her head. A grumbling roar filled the air above the pit. Dirt sprayed over her, scratching her face and sticking to the blood on the sides of her mouth. She opened her lips to call out but her words were snatched up in a whirlwind of cold air. *What if they can't see me?* Her exhausted mind raced. After fighting so hard to survive, she couldn't just lie there and let her last chance slip away.

She made another attempt to sit up but a dagger of agony sliced through her chest. Harper let her head drop back against the wet hoodie. The dirt continued to fly around her. Her mind threw up images of the witch flying though the tornado in *The Wizard of Oz*. "I'm like Dorothy," she whispered.

"Dorothy? Is that your name, sweetheart?"

Harper jerked sideways. She cried out and shrank from the male voice so near her face. Flying dirt and leaves clouded her vision. She batted at the man with her left hand. *It's him. Somehow he's freed himself and now he's going to put his hands on me.* "No. No, please don't." Harper raised her voice trying to be heard over the roar above.

"My name's Trent. I'm a police officer." His voice, calm and deep broke through her panic. "You're safe, Dorothy. We're here to help you."

Harper tried opening and closing her eyes. The dirt and debris flying around her seemed to clear, but only slightly. *Did I hear a voice or was that in my head?* She raised her left hand and groped the air. Her fingers brushed something slippery and cold. Fabric of some kind? Her hand slid over the smooth surface before becoming encased in warm flesh.

"It's alright, were going to get you out of here. You're safe." This time, there could be no mistaking what she saw. A police officer, not an apparition, held her hand.

Harper let out a long shuddering wail and squeezed the man's hand, afraid it might disappear like smoke if she let go. Other voices floated back and forth across the pit. Heavy boots crunched through the damp earth close to her head and alongside her body.

"It's okay, Dorothy, you're safe." He repeated the reassurance like a soothing mantra. Harper didn't think she'd ever tire of hearing those two words. *You're safe*.

"I'm Harper," she tried to make herself heard over the roar from above and the throng of activity surrounding her.

"What's that?" He squeezed her hand. "What did you say?"

"My name's Harper," This time her voice sounded stronger. Not quite her old self, but certainly closer.

He leaned over her, blocking the whirlwind and revealing his features. Sandy hair and blue eyes. Steady eyes – calm. "We're going to move your friend over there first. When we've got him in the helicopter, you'll go up next."

"He's not my friend," her voice trembled. "He did this." The blue eyes widened and the cop, *Trent* she thought he had said, called out to someone. His voice sounded urgent but still unfazed.

Her chest burned and her eyes felt raw, the lids weighed down as if with clumps of dirt. She let them drop. Voices buzzed senselessly. Harper fell into blackness.

* * *

Judith's legs scissored forwards ready to pick up speed. Before she'd made it two steps, her head jerked back and her body ran out from under her. Martin's fist, tangled in the back of her hair, snatched her mid-stride. Judith's back hit the ground with a thump and the air spat out of her lungs. Her mouth worked opened in a grimace trying to draw in blocked air. The sky, visible in bars through the tree tops, glowed grey and orange.

Sound rushed back with a wheezy breath. Air filled her lungs; Judith gulped it in, her chest heaving. She drew her knees up and then felt them forced down. Martin's face appeared above her blocking the sky.

"Where's my brother, you bitch?" He sat on her thighs, his weight pinning her legs. His face close to hers, she could see herself reflected in his almost black eyes.

His hand wrapped around her neck, he started to squeeze. Judith's hand pushed his chest pulling his shirt open. His bulk felt like a solid immovable wall. "What did you do to Archie?" He sprayed her with spittle.

Judith's hands dropped to her waist. She touched the front pocket of her shorts and then found the gap in the fabric. Martin's grip tightened. He shook her neck jarring her head against the dirt. "Answer me." He gave her neck another shake and then loosened his grip.

"He's near the trail," her voice a barely audible croak. Judith fumbled the penknife out of her pocket using her right hand. "He's alive, but in bad shape." Martin stared into her eyes as if trying to read her mind, decide if she was telling the truth or not.

A grinding roar echoed over the tree tops. Martin kept his hand on her throat and looked up. The moment's distraction was all she needed. Judith used both hands and pulled open the blade. Then held it flat against her stomach.

Martin turned his attention back on her, "No more fucking around. Time's up." His eyes shifted away from her face as if he didn't want to watch as he squeezed the life out of her.

The instant before his grip closed off her airway, Judith spoke, "You won't get away with this." She slid the knife up to her chest listening to the blood whoosh in her ears. A tremble travelled through her body, carried on a wave of adrenalin.

Martin looked into her eyes. One side of his mouth twitched in what might have been a grin. "I always have a back-up plan."

"So do I," she said with a rush of air and slammed the penknife into his left eye.

The blade pierced Martin's eye with a burping pop. Warm liquid squirted over Judith's fingers. He screamed, a sound somewhere between rage and agony. Martin tore his hand away from her throat and tried to reach for his face. Judith snaked her left hand around the back of his neck as if pulling him in for a kiss. Her fingers gripped the damp mass of hair on the back of his head and held him steady while she pushed the blade through his eyes socket burying it so deep that the handle slipped out of her grip.

Martin's body arched. Spittle flew out of his open mouth and splattered Judith's face. Thick yolky looking goo hung from his left eye socket. Judith gagged and pushed his body away.

He offered no resistance. His bulk flopped sideways giving her enough room to slide away from him. Judith sat up and sprang to her feet, kicking up a spray of dirt and leaves. She staggered a few steps coughing and gagging. Scratching and rustling came from behind her. She swung around expecting another attack.

Martin lay on his back, damp leaves and dirt covered the right side of his black shirt. The handle of the hunting knife surrounded by a still-spreading patch of blood protruded from his thigh. His legs jittered and drummed against the ground. The light had changed from orange to dusky grey turning the skin on his face to a pale ghoulish mask streaked with oily looking blood. Judith forced herself to look at his eye.

In the gloom, it was almost black. The lid drooped slightly turning his agonised expression into something that resembled a sleazy wink. In the centre of the pulpy mess, a glint of metal. The curved end of the penknife handle Judith realised. Another cramp seized her abdomen. She covered her mouth and instantly regretted the movement. The smell of the yolky slime on her fingers coated her nostrils. She bent at the waist and gagged out a film of clear liquid.

Judith stayed bent forward breathing deeply, trying to flush the smell of blood and bile out of her nose. When the cramps subsided, she lifted the tattered ends of her shirt and wiped her mouth and eyes. Apart from her breathing and the chirp of insects, all was silent. She risked another look at Martin, mostly to reassure herself he wasn't getting up, but also out of grim curiosity. A need to see the damage she'd done.

His legs were still, the twitching and drumming ceased. Martin's ruined face hung in the vacant slackness of death. Judith considered feeling for his pulse just make sure he was gone, but decided the memory of his face would be enough to haunt her dreams without adding the feel of his dead skin. She guessed she should feel guilt over killing him. After everything that he'd done, he was a human being. But inside she felt only hollowness. Hollowness and exhaustion.

Judith turned away and headed back towards the trail. It occurred to her that the distant sound of the helicopter had stopped. *I hope Harper's flying away from this desolate place,* she thought, and hurried forward.

* * *

The world rushed back with a roar. Harper opened her eyes and found herself looking up at grey sky and thick blue cable. The smell of fuel and grease wafted over her and the thundering whir of helicopter blades pushed against her eardrums, blocking even the sound of her own breathing. She felt weightless, tiny. She tried moving her good arm and found it bound against her body. Tilting her head up, she realised she was draped in silver and encased in a metal basket swinging through the sky. Her lips felt frozen against her teeth, her face numb with cold.

In seconds, she arrived at the opening to the helicopter and the basket was pulled into the safety of the aircraft.

The basket thumped against something. Harper's injured arm jostled against the side of the cage. A shaft of pain ripped through her, starting at her wrist and travelling like electricity up her arm. She gasped and clamped her teeth together.

"Sorry, love. We've got you now. All steady from here," came a man's voice, loud and clear over the roar of the blades. His face appeared over her. Not Trent, but someone younger with the sort of pale freckled skin that looked like it would burn in seconds if exposed to the sun. "I'm Matt, I'm a medic. You're safe." He held her gaze and nodded. "Where's the pain?"

Harper's mind felt sluggish. Even answering the simplest questions required thought. "Arm... arm and chest."

He nodded and turned away. She heard clanging and plastic tearing. When he turned back, he held a small plastic mask.

"Where's Judith and Milly?" She raised her head and craned her neck.

"The police are still down there." He reached forward stretching the elastic strap of the mask towards her head.

"No." Her voice sounded harsh. "I don't want to leave without them." Pain cut through her chest and she felt something bubbling in her throat. "I can't…"

"We're not leaving them behind, but we need to get you and this guy to hospital." He jerked his head to the right. "He's in pretty bad shape. We can't hang about."

Harper turned her head to the right. Archie lay only a few metres away strapped to an identical cage. Two people Harper guessed were medics huddled over him. *Do they know what he did?* It wouldn't matter; these people would help him no matter what. She was about to say something, warn them about him, when the mask clamped over her nose and mouth.

"Don't try to talk. Just breathe." Matt's voice had a soothing quality. Harper wanted to close her eyes and fall back into the blackness. But Judith and Milly were still down there. So was Martin. She had to tell them. Tell them to get on their radio and get the police to find Judith and Milly before it was too late.

"They'll find them." Matt spoke as if he'd heard her thoughts. "They won't stop until your friends are safe."

"Not my friend, my love," her lips moved behind the mask.

"He's crashing," came another voice nearby, sharp and urgent. The word set off a flurry of movement.

Harper heard packages being torn open and orders barked. She could make no further sense of what they said, but the critical nature of their conversation was clear to her even as she drifted into unconsciousness. *I hope he dies*, she thought and gave in to the darkness.

* * *

A light mist drifted across the ground, winding its way through trees and shrubs. Judith felt the temperature dipping as dusk bled into evening. She wrapped her arms around herself, trying to block the chill that eked its way through her flesh and into her bones. Her teeth chattered and her legs felt numb both from cold and fatigue.

It had been at least fifteen minutes since she'd noticed the helicopter's absence – a good sign. They must have found Harper or they'd still be searching. But did that mean the rescue party had gone? *No, surely not.* She'd told the triple-zero operator how many people needed help; they wouldn't just leave. Would they? The thought of spending another night in the Leeuwin-Naturaliste National Park sparked a wave of panic.

I can't stay out here alone, not with Martin. She stopped moving and looked over her shoulder. The wilderness, draped in mist and shadows looked menacing and desolate. It was easy to imagine Martin lurching out of the trees, empty eye socket filled with blood and lips drawn back in murderous hate. Her skin crawled with goose bumps. She turned back and forced her quivering legs on.

It was difficult to be sure how much farther she'd need to walk before reaching the spot where she'd found Harper. When Judith left, all she could think about was finding her sister. She cursed herself for not taking more notice of landmarks and distances. It would be full dark soon and Judith had no idea if she headed in the right direction. A cold, hard lump of panic formed in the pit of her stomach. She tried to talk herself through the fear by recounting what she could remember of the landmarks.

There had been an open space with deep grass, she remembered crossing the clearing before entering the trees. *Yes, yes. I crossed that clearing at least twenty minutes ago.* Before the clearing there'd been… Her memory faltered. She wanted to stop and rest. Her mind refused to work as if the mist covering the landscape had worked its way inside her head to blanket her thoughts. Her scratched and bruised thighs burned with the effort of climbing the slope. Judith looked down at her legs and her mouth dropped open.

The slope. The scratches. She'd walked down the slope and into a thick crop of bushes. Heading upwards meant she had to be moving in the right direction. Licking her cracked lips, she bent forward and half-walked, half-crawled her way over the rocky slope. Her fingers clawed at the ground splitting and breaking what remained of her fingernails.

A bird called from higher ground. The sound deep and long, like an echoing voice. Judith scrambled upwards wondering what sort of bird made such a human sound. The call drifted over the slope and seemed to repeat from both right and left.

"Scary bir..." Judith muttered and then caught her breath. Listening, she didn't blink or move. This time the call came from the right, clear and booming.

"Judith?"

She dropped to the ground flattening herself against the uneven surface. Her chin, already raw from bashing against the cliff, bounced off a flat stone half-buried in the slope. Judith winced and bit her lip. *Is it him, Archie? He could have been faking, pretending to be badly hurt. What if he's looking for me?* She lifted her head and sucked in air. *No*, she reminded herself. *I heard the helicopter, they must have found him. Yeah, but what if they didn't?*

Judith knew Archie couldn't possibly be running around calling her name. She'd seen the back of his head and how his skull dipped inwards, but she couldn't shake the fear. Shivering, she clung to the ground digging her fingers into the damp earth. Pressing her check against the dirt, she considered running. Maybe hiding amongst the trees. Her mind threw up images of Archie, one eye bulging and dark blood dripping down his neck, climbing over the slope on his hands and knees.

Making a decision on what to do next drove a wedge of panic through her chest. She hesitated, caught between hope and dread. Tears blurred her vision.

The call came again, this time closer, "Judith?" A pause and then more.

"Judith?" Her name repeated over and over like a chant coming from all directions.

She raised her head. Archie might be evil, but he couldn't be in five places at once. The calls came from multiple people. It hit her like a cold wind. *A search party*. It was so obvious she almost laughed. Clambering to her knees, she pushed herself up, stumbled, and then managed to stand.

"I'm here," her voice came out so thin and high she hardly recognised it as her own. She gulped in air and pressed her hand against her stomach. "Help!" The word burst out with all the power she could muster. Judith sucked in another breath and continued to call, "Help. Help. Help." She repeated the cry until her bruised and battered throat refused to work.

Lights poured over the slope. A rush of voices and movement. Judith stood and waited for the glow of torches to find her. The first to reach her, a man carrying a torch and a nylon shoulder bag, rushed forward pinning her in his light.

"You're okay," he said, his voice overly loud and breathless. He dropped the bag and pulled out a silver blanket which he draped around her shoulders. Judith swayed as if the light blanket might topple her over. The man's arm shot out and encircled her waist. "I've got you, love." His voice, heavy with concern and reassurance seemed to pull at something in her head and stomach. Whatever thin strands of control and resolve that remained, broke and she began to sob.

More people approached. The man holding her said his name was Frank.

"Don't let go, Frank," she croaked out around sobs.

"I won't, love," he said simply, and began walking her over the slope.

* * *

Judith woke not with a start but a slow return to the world. She lay on her side in a private room of Bunbury Hospital. A thin bar of light, pale and grey fell across the green linoleum floor. Her hands were covered in small dressings. They'd been washed clean of dirt and grit, but her nails were shredded and lined with grime. The roof of her mouth dusty with thirst, she sat up reluctantly leaving the warm comfort of the pillows. Her back spasmed and the muscles in her thighs and calves groaned.

She reached for the plastic beaker on the bedside trolley and took a sip of water. Her throat clenched, squeezing the cool liquid over what felt like bits of wire lining her tonsils. Her head throbbed, most likely from the sleeping pills she'd been given the night before.

After everything that had happened, Judith expected to feel ... What? She wasn't sure, but certainly not ready to laugh about her ordeal. But why not? She was alive and so was Harper. They'd come through a nightmare, wasn't that something to be celebrated? Almost as quickly as the spark of relief grew, it burned out in a blaze of guilt. *Milly.*

Judith ran her fingers through her hair, it felt stiff with grime. She wondered if the police had found her sister yet or if she still lying near that tree looking up at the sky with misty eyes. The door clanged open. Judith jumped and grabbed the sheets, clenching them up to her chest.

"Morning," a tiny woman in black pants and a navy shirt sang. She carried a tray out in front of her. She approached the bed, her round hips swaying, and placed the tray on the trolley.

Judith picked up the smell of toast and coffee. Her stomach groaned. A nurse offered her a sandwich last night, but her throat had been too tender to attempt food. But sore throat or not, she intended to eat whatever she could force past her tonsils.

"You want tea or coffee?" The woman asked with a smile that seemed too bright for such and early hour.

Fifteen minutes later Judith put down her spoon. She'd worked her way through a banana flavoured yoghurt, a blueberry muffin, and two cups of coffee. Her body might still be racked with aches and pains, but at least her stomach felt calm. The food seemed to have also restored some of her strength. She tossed the covers aside and flung her legs over the edge of the bed.

After a brief visit to the bathroom, where a haunted woman with brown Betadine stains dotted over her cut and swollen face greeted her in the mirror, Judith returned to the bed. She wanted to see Harper. That was her priority. Next, find some clothes and check herself out of the hospital.

She grabbed the nurse's call button and was about to press it when a woman in black pants and a white zip-front top appeared. "Morning. I'll just check your vitals." The woman announced and lifted the chart from the end of the bed. She began bustling around, taking Judith's blood pressure and writing on the chart. 'Susan' was printed in bold black letters on a name badge pinned to her ample chest.

Susan dropped the chart back into the cage at the end of the bed. "How's your pain level?" she asked, slipping her pen in the pocket just above her badge.

Judith shook her head. "I want to see Harper." The words came out louder than she'd intended. Nurse Susan stopped talking and finally made eye contact. Her thin brown eyebrows drew together. "Sorry, I just… I've been…" Suddenly she didn't know what to say. How could she possibly explain her need to see Harper in a way that made sense to a complete stranger? "Harper Sydney, my girlfriend." She tried again. "She was brought in last night. I just need to see her… Make sure she's alright and knows I'm here."

The woman's broad face softened. She was younger than Judith first thought, maybe thirty or so. "I heard about what happened." Her shoulders dropped and she let out a breath. "Well, some of it." She pushed the trolley away and sat on the bed beside Judith. "Your girlfriend has had surgery and she's doing well."

"Is she…"

"I don't have any details, just what I've heard so don't quote me on any of it." She shifted slightly to look Judith in the eyes. Her face was clear and unlined except for her forehead which wrinkled when she talked. "When I got to work this morning, there were reporters outside the hospital. The staff have been warned not to talk to any of them. We've been given a run down on what happened." She hesitated. "I'm not supposed to even be discussing any of it with *you*." She rolled her eyes. "I'm supposed to refer your questions to the doctor on duty." She made a clicking sound with her tongue. "What a load of rubbish. You two have been through enough without making you sit here wringing your hands waiting for information you should be entitled to."

"Thank you." Judith felt a surge of gratitude towards the nurse. "When can I see her?"

Susan let out another long breath and stood. "That, I don't know." She checked her watch. "It's nearly eight-thirty. I've been told the police will be in to see you this morning and the doctor will be around soon. They'll be able to tell you more." She pulled the hem of her white smock down around her hips. "Now, let's concentrate on making sure *you're* okay."

She seemed to be waiting for a response. "Yes. Okay." Judith managed a weak smile, it pulled on her grazed cheek making her wince.

"I'll give you a couple of paracetamol, they'll help with the aches and pains. In the meantime, sit tight and I'll pop my head in and let you know if I hear anything."

Judith swallowed a string of protest that threatened to burst from her. Alienating Susan, a young nurse trying to be kind, wouldn't help the situation. At least she had a little more information. Harper was doing well. Not much, but it would keep her going until she got through the morning.

An hour and a half later, her already raw throat felt as if she'd swallowed a ball of wire. She'd answered questions and recounted the events of the last two days at least twice. Two police detectives, one in his fifties with a shaved head and bushy eyebrows, the other younger and blonde, conducted the interview at her bedside. Of the two, the younger man, Detective Branstrum did most of the talking.

"You say you left your sister with one of the men who later turned out to be Martin Crowell." His eyes, pale blue and deeply set, drifted from Judith to his note book. "What happened then?" His voice was calm, almost gentle.

Judith frowned. Even the slightest movement pulled at every cut and scrape on her face. "You already asked me that." She leaned back against the pillows and closed her eyes. The room smelled of Betadine and cleaning chemicals. The odour reminded her of sickness. "Why do you want to hear the same things over and over again?" Even as she asked the question, she knew the answer. They wanted to check her story. If she was lying, her answers might change. "I'm telling you the truth." She clasped her hand to her throat as if she could ease the words out. "Martin and Archie Crowell terrorised us. Martin killed my sister and Archie told me he murdered my mother." Her voice broke and tears ran down her cheeks. "I can't keep doing this."

Branstrum stepped forward and grabbed a box of tissues off the bedside locker. "I'm sorry, Ms Birdsworth," he said holding out the box. "I'm not trying to upset you."

"I don't want a fucking tissue," Judith rasped and then snatched the box. She pulled out a handful of tissues and swiped at her eyes. "I want to see Harper. I want to know where my…" She sucked in a breath to steady her voice. "I want to know where my sister is. Is she here?"

Rather than being offended by her outburst, Branstrum's tight expression softened. He slipped his notebook in the back pocket of his pants. "The search party set out at first light. As soon as they find her, I'll let you know."

Find her. That meant Milly had been out in the forest all night. Judith shuddered. Suddenly the room, small and clinical, lit by milky morning light, seemed surreal. She felt as though the whole scene were a mirage and any minute she'd open her eyes and be back in the forest running for her life.

She tried to focus on Branstrum. His mouth moved, but the words were a jumble. "What?"

Branstrum looked at his partner. It was a quick movement, but something in the look unsettled her. She had the feeling he was getting ready to deliver bad news. *Can it get any worse?* After what she'd seen *and* done, she decided not to ponder that question.

"Archie Crowell was transported to Royal Perth Hospital last night. He's undergoing neurosurgery. I don't know his condition, but I can tell you he was briefly conscious when I spoke to him in the early hours."

Judith shook her head. "Did you see that old man?" She searched for his name, "William. Did you see what that animal did to him? To Harper?" She looked from Branstrum to his partner. Their faces were unreadable. "I don't care what happens to Archie. Why would I?"

"I understand," Branstrum's voice remained calm, solemn. "When I spoke to him, he claimed to have no memory of what took place on the trails in and around the Leeuwin-Naturaliste National Park. In fact," he went on, "he claims to have no memory of ever being in your mother's house or conspiring with his brother to harm you." He shrugged. "If he survives the surgery *and* he's ever fit to stand trial, apart from some physical evidence on the knife..." His pale blue eyes regarded her intently. "Our case against him will come down to your testimony. Yours and Ms Sydney's."

Judith let the detective's words sink in. Archie might never have to pay for what he'd done. That was the bottom line. "What are you telling me? That he might get away with it?" She tried to keep the anger out of her voice.

"What I'm trying to tell you, Ms Birdsworth is that we need to build a rock-solid case against him and that means you can't talk to Ms Sydney until we've taken her statement."

"But I have to…"

He held up his hand to silence her. "And, since she's still recovering from surgery, I won't press her for a statement until later this afternoon."

Judith opened her mouth to object, but he continued speaking. "I can, however, let you see her with an officer present. I'll have a constable here within the hour." He turned to his partner.

"I'll get someone sent over." It was the first time the other man spoke. Judith tried to recall his name. Morris or Norris, she couldn't quite remember. He gave her a nod and left the room.

The door closed behind the older detective with a squeak of rubber on linoleum. For a moment there was silence save the babble of voices from the corridor. Branstrum's gaze remained fixed on the window where olive green curtains framed the morning sky. Judith wondered if the "million miles" stare was another police tactic – say nothing and wait for the guilty party to fill the silence. Another thought quickly followed, *I am guilty. I wanted to get Milly out there and scare the truth out of her. Now three people are dead.*

She looked up surprised to see the detective's pale eyes trained on her. Her face burned hot with shame. Judith dropped her eyes and regarded her shredded finger nails. *He can see the guilt written all over my face.* She tried to think of something to say, but her mind filled with images of her sister falling. The sound of Milly's head hitting the ground reverberated in her ears making her jerk back against the pillows.

"Are you alright?" Branstrum's voice seemed calm. His next words stunned her. "I know what you're thinking."

Her mouth dropped open. She could hear her own heart beating with unnerving clarity. *Did he read my face? How can he know what I feel?* She had the urge to drop her gaze again but resisted it. Everything she'd told him was true. She'd left nothing out, even the part about planning to scare her sister. Yet pinned under his unwavering eyes, she felt like a criminal.

"You feel guilty."

Judith let out a sharp breath and gripped the sheet with her battered hands. "I set all this in motion. I opened the door to those two ... maniacs. My sister's dead. How should I feel?"

His brow wrinkled and the stony eyes softened. "I've been doing this a long time. Maybe too long." He shrugged, it was a tired movement. "Archie Crowell is a killer. Not a murderer or a lunatic, but a killer. Based on experience, I know the difference between murders and killers. Archie is the latter. He takes lives not for vengeance or gain but because it's his nature to kill." He returned his gaze to the window. "I met someone like him years ago when I was just starting out in this job. I questioned him about an assault in custody. He'd been in prison for years by then, convicted of a string of murders. Quite infamous." Branstrum let out a long breath. "A serial killer. We don't have many of those in Western Australia. Not that we've caught anyway. Archie reminded me of him." His voice changed, became more conversational. "It wasn't anything he said or did, just an absence of humanity." He hesitated as if trying to find the right words. Judith felt a cold finger creep up her spine. "It's like being close to a deep quarry filled with black water. When you lean in, all you feel is ... desolation." He turned back to Judith. "You're not responsible for the death of your sister *or* William Walterson. The idiotic plan you had to scare your sister didn't kill her. Archie Crowell and his brother did that without any help from you. Remember that." He waggled his finger at her in a comical way, but there was no humour in his voice.

Judith nodded, not sure what to say. Branstrum looked at his watch. "What the hell's keeping Norris?" He was all business again.

As if waiting for his cue, Norris elbowed the door open. "The locals are sending a constable over. She'll be here in ten." The chipper voice didn't quite match the shaved head. Judith fleetingly wondered if the older detective kept his head shaved to shift the attention off his voice.

"Nice one." Branstrum nodded to his partner. To Judith he said, "When you see Ms Sydney, don't discuss anything that happened out there." He raised his blonde eyebrows. "Clear?"

"Clear," Judith echoed.

* * *

A small window at the far end of Harper's room shed a pool of weak light which didn't quite reach the bed. The space felt crowded even though the only occupants apart from Harper, were Judith and a female uniformed officer. Constable Tarrant as she'd introduced herself, took up a position in front of the window. In doing so, she blocked much of the natural light.

Dressed in a set of washed out blue scrubs provided by Susan, Judith approached the bed. Harper's small body looked shrunken under the covers. As if the ordeal of the last few days had used her up. Her right arm encased in a thick layer of brown and white bandages, lay along her body.

Harper's eyes flicked open. There was panic and pain in the expression that crossed her face. It reminded Judith of a rescue dog she'd seen on TV. She remembered thinking the animal looked haunted, as if expecting a blow with each sound.

"It's me, sweetheart." She tried to keep her voice even.

Harper didn't respond. Her gaze drifted through Judith as if seeing something distant and unrecognisable. Judith moved closer, positioning herself near Harper's head. "It's Judith," she tried again.

The nurse warned her that Harper had been given pain medication and might be unresponsive, but nothing had prepared Judith for the dull look in her partner's eyes. Judith pressed her hand to the side of Harper's face. Her skin felt warm and smooth. She blinked and her expression changed. It was as if the touch had brought her to the surface of whatever misty land she'd been inhabiting. Her eyes filled with tears and her face crumpled.

"Jude?" Her uninjured hand gripped Judith's shoulder. "They told me you were alive, but ..." Her words faltered as if she were having difficulty drawing breath. "I didn't know if I'd only dreamt it."

Judith chuckled, "You know me, I keep on keeping on." She brushed a strand of golden hair away from Harper's face. "I'm not going anywhere. It's all over now and we're together."

The corners of Harper's mouth turned up in the beginnings of a smile. For a second, Judith saw the light behind her girlfriend's eyes turn back on. Then a shadow crossed her pale face. "Milly?"

Judith felt the now familiar ache of loss. She tried to put her thoughts into words that would explain what happened. In the end, she settled for a shake of her head.

Harper let out a trembling breath and closed her eyes. Fresh tears streamed down her cheeks running over Judith's hand like warm ribbons. She felt Harper's hand squeeze her shoulder. There would be time for explanations later. *We got through two days in hell*, Judith reminded herself. *We can get through this*.

Chapter Twenty-Nine

Harper tapped a finger to her lips and watched Judith's white BMW Sport drive away. The car negotiated its way around the curving private road and disappeared from view. The winery near Margaret River reminded her of an English castle. With rolling lawns, rows of perfectly-trained rose bushes alive with spring and elegant clusters of vines, the winery seemed other-worldly in its perfection and tranquillity. Despite the serene setting, she felt a quiver of dread. A now familiar feeling.

In the four months since her ordeal in the National Park, Harper found herself struggling with bouts of anxiety. Most common when alone, the attacks would rise up and smother her with terror and helplessness. The episodes, that's what her psychologist called them, began shortly after she was released from the hospital. Harper remembered the first time the terror hit.

Judith had rented a cabin along the beach in Yallingup so that Harper would have somewhere to recuperate for a few days before they drove back to Perth. Less than a week after their encounter with the Crowell brothers, late autumn marched towards winter. The outlook turned from cloudy to bleak.

***

Harper, wrapped in a red checked blanket, sat on the cabin's back deck overlooking an endless stretch of white sandy beach.

"How's the arm?" Judith set down a mug of tea on the small wooden side table. The graze on her cheek had formed into a large brown scab. A network of bruises ringed her neck like angry blue fingers.

"Thanks." Harper nodded at the cup. She didn't remember asking for it, but that's not to say she hadn't. The pain medication they'd given her at the hospital kept her feeling off balance and dreamy. "It's aching a bit, not too bad."

She reached for the cup with her left hand and winced. Three broken ribs and a punctured lung had a far more debilitating effect than her broken arm. Every movement brought a shaft of pain. Even motionless and on pain relief, it felt as if a thick rubber band had been wrapped around her chest, squeezing her lungs.

Judith remained standing, one elbow on the railing that encircled the deck. She regarded Harper. In the soft afternoon light, she looked relaxed. The lines of worry that criss-crossed the corners of her eyes smoothed away. "Even after everything that's happened. I still feel drawn to this place …" She seemed to want to say more but let her words trail off and turned towards the ocean.

"I know what you mean." Judith looked over her shoulder. The sea breeze ruffled her bouncy brown hair, plastering it around her cheeks.

She smiled. It was a moment Harper hoped she'd remember for ever. The two of them, battered and bruised but slowly coming back to life.

"How about fish and chips?" Judith chuckled. "I'm starving and you need the stodge."

Five minutes later, Judith, bundled up in a puffy grey jacket, remerged on the deck. "I'm going to walk to the chip shop. I won't be long."

"Okay." The rush of the surf was almost hypnotic. Harper felt sleepy but didn't have the energy to move.

"Will you be alright out here until I get back?" Harper could tell Judith was making an effort to keep her tone light, but an edge of worry had still crept in.

"Right as rain," Harper smiled up at her. "If anyone asks how you hurt your face, tell them you fell off an elephant in Thailand."

Judith's face relaxed. "That's a very plausible story. Thanks for that." She bent forward and kissed Harper on the lips. She smelled of lemon scented shampoo. "Do you want chocolate or an ice-cream?"

Harper shook her head. "I've got everything I need."

"Okay. Be back in twenty."

The front door had thudded closed. Harper picked up the mug of tea and took a sip. The hot liquid warmed her throat and a cloud of steam wafted over her chilled face. The breeze blew in off the ocean with a frigid blast, flapping the folds of the blanket against her neck. Although the thought of moving seemed like a gargantuan effort, she decided it might be time to go inside.

Harper returned the mug to the table and rose gingerly to her feet. The wind had picked up, whipping her hair around and flapping the blanket. She took a last look at the beach and froze. A figure walked the shore line a hundred metres or so in the distance. She felt a hollow sensation in the pit of her stomach.

Even though the shape was far away, she could tell it was a man. *Was he there all along?* Her mind snapped out of the dreamy haze. *Maybe he was watching and saw Judith leave.* A set of steep wooden stairs led from the deck down to the sand. Harper bit her lip, there was nothing to stop him walking right up to the cabin. *Why did we rent a place so exposed?*

She snapped her head around searching for people on the sand. Apart from the rush of the surf and the occasional cry of gulls, the beach looked deserted. *No,* she corrected herself. *He's here*. All sorts of possibilities flooded her imagination. Her vision grew narrow. The approaching figure filled her view.

Harper spun around twisting her battered torso. Battling the pain that sliced across her ribs, she bolted for the sliding door. Once inside, she slammed it closed with enough force to rattle the thickened glass. Clicking the small latch, she cursed under her breath. *This place is no safer than hiding in the grass trees in the National Park*. The thought brought back horrific images of Archie plunging the knife into William's neck. Harper moaned and headed for the bathroom.

Each step sent rivulets of fire up her body and through her arm. Her feet, clad only in fluffy socks, slipped and slid as she tried to find purchase on the highly polished timber floor. She rounded the corner leading to the hallway and her right foot slid back and out from under her. Her knee hit the floor and her injured arm, encased in layers of bandages and a sling, collided with the wall.

For a few seconds, the world turned white. Harper's teeth clamped together and her head strained backwards as if pulling away from the agony that threatened to swallow her entire being. She clamped her left hand around her injured arm and rocked back and forth.

"Oh God. Oh God." The words came out around rapid-fire breathing.

In spite of the pain, her mind could only focus on escape. From what, she wasn't quite sure. The one thing that seemed certain, she was in danger. The man on the beach, he looked like Archie. At least from a distance. But in that moment, it didn't matter who he was. He was there and she was alone.

"No. No. No." Harper clambered to her feet. *Run or hide? Run or hide?*

* * *

When Judith returned fifteen minutes later, she found Harper in the shower stall sobbing.

Since then, the anxiety attacks had become a new and debilitating aspect of her life. It was only Judith's endless patience and encouragement that stopped Harper losing her mind and becoming a shut-in.

She thought of Judith and her face drew tight with worry. Even through the blanket of self-involvement she'd covered herself in, Harper could see the changes in her once calm and down-to-earth girlfriend. Judith had taken to over-exercising. At first, Harper thought it was her way of relieving stress and working through the trauma. But as the months went by, Judith spent more and more time working out. Hours running on the treadmill and lifting weights had turned Judith's trim frame into a mass of sinew and muscle.

Harper tried to talk to her about it, but Judith always laughed it off. "I'm not getting any younger. I've got to keep in shape so you don't run off with some pretty young thing."

But Harper could see through the trite remarks. Judith worked her body like a fighter getting ready for the match of her life. Always at home because Harper hated to be left alone. *I'm part of the stress*, Harper thought bitterly. *I'm always terrified and she's trying to turn herself into super woman for me.* But self-knowledge meant nothing when the panic set in and she couldn't hide her fear.

Now, standing at the grand entrance to one of the most breath-taking wineries in the South West, she felt the familiar claws of terror shredding her gut. Her inner voice whispered warnings, urging her to run. She battled against the desire to bolt down the private road and hide somewhere until she could phone Judith.

A fine sheen of sweat broke out on Harper's forehead. Her lips felt dry and rubbery. The parking lot to the side of the sprawling building was at half capacity. *So many people*, Harper wondered if one of the diners might be watching her. Maybe crouched down behind a car. *What am I doing here?* She became certain that the meeting was a bad idea. What good would it do to relive what happened?

"Hello, you must be Harper." Her heart jumped before her mind recognised the voice belonged to a woman.

"Sorry. Did I startle you?" The woman asked, no doubt noticing Harper's terrified expression.

"No. I mean yes." Harper took a deep breath and tried again. "Yes, I'm Harper." Looking into the woman's calm green eyes framed by red rimmed spectacles, the panic began to subside. "I'm glad you came."

The woman nodded. "I'm Rebecca Walterson. Shall we go in?"

Rebecca asked for a table on the terrace overlooking the vineyard. Once they were seated, an awkward silence settled. Harper searched for something to say, but where did she begin? Fortunately, the waitress arrived and saved her from the problem.

"I'd like a glass of white wine," Rebecca told the waitress. Turning her attention to Harper, she asked, "Will you join me?"

Her voice, the formality with which she spoke, like an echo of those moments Harper spent with the woman's father, William.

"Yes, thank you." Harper could feel herself relaxing. It seemed like an eternity since she'd really relaxed.

"This place," Rebecca said a moment later, waving her long, slim arm towards the gardens. "It really is quite lovely. My father enjoyed dining at the local wineries. *Civilised* he called them." She gave a wistful smile. "I suppose he was right."

The table was draped in a thick white cloth. A small bowl of freesia sat in the centre. The sweet fresh scent reminded Harper of something she'd almost forgotten.

"When I met your father, I noticed he smelled of humbugs." Harper laughed nervously. "I'd almost forgotten that until just now."

Rebecca grimaced. "Oh how those humbugs annoyed my mother." The grimace turned into a smile that lit up her otherwise sharp features. "She'd always tease him about the sucking sounds he made. What a pair they were." She shook her head and her muddy blonde bob bounced against her jawline.

When she spoke again, her expression turned sombre. "I do miss them." She pushed her glasses up onto the bridge of her nose. "What is it you want to talk to me about, Harper? I'm sure it's not what sort of sweets my father ate."

It was the moment she'd been dreading and at the same time needing. Harper took a breath before answering. She looked down at the table and swallowed. "I'm here for a few reasons. First, I wanted to say sorry for not coming to the funeral. I won't make excuses. It was selfish of me not to show up." When she looked up, Rebecca's eyes were trained on her. She reminded Harper of a librarian, sensible and no-nonsense in her white blouse and camel-coloured cardigan. "I should have been there." Harper bit her lip and waited for Rebecca to answer.

She surprised her by reaching across the table and patting Harper's left hand. Her fingers were long and elegant, like her father's. "What a goose you are. Fretting over that." She gave Harper's hand a light squeeze and then let go and pushed her glasses up her nose. "The police told me some of what happened to you and your partner." She folded her arms around her thin frame. "Surviving something so horrific is not just a physical challenge, it takes every bit of strength you have just to push through each day and not let the ghosts take over."

Harper watched Rebecca's face as she spoke. The look in her eyes when she talked about ghosts reminded

Harper of her own expression. A raw look she saw regularly staring out from the bathroom mirror. She wondered what haunted Rebecca. Judging by the steel in her voice when she talked about pushing through each day, Harper guessed it must be something horrific. Losing her father to such a violent death, how that must have added to her burden.

"I hope meeting me like this isn't making things worse for you?"

Before Rebecca had a chance to answer, the waitress approached with their meals.

"Mmm. It looks marvellous." Rebecca picked up her knife and fork. "This *is* a treat. My father and I lunched together regularly. At least once a week. After he retired of course." She seemed about to say something else, but hesitated.

They ate in silence for a while, before Rebecca spoke. "Tell me, what is it you want to get off your chest?"

Harper put her fork down. "I wanted to tell you about the moments I spent with your father. I only knew him briefly but he's been on my mind so much lately." Harper took a sip of wine. The sharp tanginess tasted fresh and clean. "He came along when I was at my most terrified and desperate." She could feel a tightness in her throat. She took another swallow of wine, determined not to let herself cry. She'd done too much of that over the last four months.

"I don't know how much the police told you, but I just wanted you to know how kind and brave he was." She looked down at her plate afraid that if she met Rebecca's eyes, so like her father's, she'd lose control. "He took care of me and when …" She took a shaky breath. "And when Archie came along. He stepped in front of me." Now the tears built in her eyes. "He'd only just met me, but her told me to get behind him and stepped between me and a madman with a knife." Harper could feel her whole body trembling. "It's the bravest thing I've ever seen. I wanted you to know that."

Harper swiped at her eyes and looked up. Rebecca's eyes were shiny with tears but a wan smile creased her face. "Thank you, dear." She sniffed. "Look at us. Two women crying over their lunch, talking about how brave and wonderful he was. He would have loved it."

Harper laughed and sniffed. It was kind of funny. Funny and lovely. She found herself feeling an unexpected pang of affection for William's daughter. And with that realisation came a little spark of happiness. The anxiety that had loomed over her for four months like a dark bird, shifted. It didn't fly away, maybe just ruffled its wing as if *thinking* about taking flight.

"A toast," Rebecca said raising her glass. "To a gentle man from another time." She paused. "And the women who adored him."

Harper picked up her wine glass and clinked it against Rebecca's. "To William."

An hour later, they made their way to the parking lot, walking slowly savouring the spring sunshine. When they paused to say good bye, Harper turned her face up to the sun. She felt warm and relaxed, unburdened by dread or panic.

"Well," Rebecca said, searching through her handbag. "I'd best be off." She nodded to Harper's arm still clad in a thick nylon splint. "I hope everything's healing as it should."

"Yes." Harper looked down at her arm. "Two surgeries and a lengthy rehabilitation. William was spot on."

"He usually was. Aha, found them." Rebecca held up her car keys.

"He said it was nothing a strong, healthy girl like me couldn't manage." She touched the splint wondering if William had overestimated her ability to heal.

"As I said, he was usually right." Then as if reading Harper's mind, she added. "Trust his prognosis, he was a very good judge of character."

Harper nodded. She wanted to believe she had the strength to leave the fear in the past and focus on the future. Maybe Rebecca was right, Harper had to trust not just William's belief in her, but her own.

"Judith and I are looking for a property here in Margaret River. When we get settled would you like to have dinner with us?"

A smile lit up Rebecca's face and changed her features from sharp to radiant. "I'd love to. Now, I must fly." With that, she loped off towards the parking lot.

When Judith pulled up five minutes later, Harper realised she hadn't thought about being alone in the carpark.

Chapter Thirty

Nora Coates twirled a ball-point pen between her fingers and flipped through a stack of patient notes. Of the one hundred and twenty beds in the Fiona Stanley Rehabilitation Centre, ninety-six were currently occupied. Not quite filled to capacity but getting there. Nora checked the clock over the nurses' station against her wrist watch: 6:55 pm. Her shift didn't officially begin until seven o'clock, but she made a habit of getting in a bit early and checking the notes. It gave her a better idea of what the evening shift held.

Evenings were quiet in the centre, almost peaceful. Despite the unsociable hours, Nora preferred working at night. Besides, with Joe long gone and her daughter married and living in Sydney, the house seemed emptier at night. By the time her shift started, physio and group sessions had finished for the day. With the evening meals out of the way, the only traffic consisted of a few last minute visitors. *Alright*, she told herself. *You've put it off for long enough.* She slapped down the pen and picked up Archie Crowell's file.

Nora knew it was ridiculous, bordering on unprofessional even, but the patient in room 81 gave her the creeping jitters. *It's all in your head*, she reminded herself. Yet each time she approached his room, her stomach would shrivel up like a soggy Kleenex. *You've heard the stories about what he did and you've built him up in to some kind of Hannibal Lecter. He's only twenty-four, for God's sake.* But no matter how many times she tried to put her feelings in perspective, she couldn't shake the fear that wrapped around her like a snake whenever she found herself in Archie's room.

She rubbed her hands together and opened the file. As expected, Archie had made little progress. The commotion of shift change-over ramped up around her as ward nurses arrived for the evening.

"How you doing, darl?" Lorna Simms brushed past Nora's chair and dumped her oversized handbag on the desk.

"Pretty good," Nora looked over her shoulder and gave the woman a brief smile. "Just reading through the notes before I start."

"Well, I need a coffee. Didn't get a wink of sleep today." As Lorna prattled on about her selfish husband and two noisy kids, Nora's attention wandered back to Archie.

His stint in the centre was nothing more than a mandated step in the process to committing him to permanent ongoing care. *Somewhere far away from here,* Nora thought. Then, *when did I become such a nasty cow?* She knew exactly when, *the day that creep show rolled in.* It wasn't like her to think about one of her patients in that way. She'd been nursing for almost thirty years and in that time she'd dealt with some real slugs. But in Nora's experience, most of the abusive or demanding behaviour could be put down to one of four things: pain, fear, substance abuse or mental illness. She wanted to believe Archie fell into the final category, but that didn't quite explain the man lying in the room three doors down from where she sat.

Archie *was* most likely mentally ill, of that Nora felt quite sure. The resident psych visited him often enough so there had to be something. But madness didn't quite gel. She was no psych, but she'd been around enough mentally ill patients to know the signs and in her opinion, Archie didn't fit the bill. He was a different kettle of fish from anyone she'd nursed. *Maybe that's why he scares me.* Or *maybe I'm too old for this place?*

She'd been thinking a lot lately about her friend Angie. She made the move from general nursing two years ago and now worked in a nursing home in Subiaco. According to Angie, she'd never been happier. The work was dull compared to being in a large public hospital and the patients never got any better, but maybe dull was what Nora needed as she approached her fiftieth birthday.

"They're all yours." Lance Borrows shrugged into his jacket. "I'm off."

"Oh. Okay." Her thoughts had been so focused on Archie, she barely noticed the comings and goings. "Err, Lance." She paused not sure how to ask the question. "Did everything go alright today?"

Lance had only been nursing for three years and still viewed every patient with an intense optimism that Nora barely remembered. "Yeah." He shrugged his narrow shoulders, moving them up and down in a jerky shift. "Doctor Jones was a bit shitty because we were two nurses short and he had to help reinsert a catheter." He pushed his bike helmet down on his shiny, bald head and clipped the straps under his chin. "Not much else going on. Except…" He paused and looked around then lowered his voice. "I heard Lisa's husband walked out on her. Poor girl." He grimaced exposing a row of slightly crooked teeth. "Don't say anything to her though, she doesn't want to talk about it."

"No. No. I won't. Hmm, that's a shame." Nora nodded. "I meant did everything go alright with," she paused and jerked her head towards the rooms. "Him?"

"Oh." Lance stretched out the word. "You mean our little friend in 81."

Nora nodded again, this time with more vigour. "Yes. Him." Getting Lance to the point bordered on painful. She began to wish she'd never asked. Not to mention the real risk that he'd now tell everyone that Nora kept asking about Archie. She was about to tell the young ward nurse to forget what she asked when he said something that sent shiver down her spine.

"He asked about you."

"What'd he say?" She heard the alarm in her voice and immediately moderated her tone. "I mean what did he ask?"

Lance chuckled. "He asked me where you lived."

Nora could feel her stomach curling in on itself. "What did you tell him?" She tried to keep her tone light, but the words came out too fast.

Lance held up both his hands motioning her to settle down. "Don't worry, I don't know where you live and even if I did, I wouldn't tell *him*. Besides," Lance said zipping up his hi-vis jacket. "It's not like he can get up and visit you."

No, Lance was right. With the catastrophic brain injury Archie had sustained, he'd probably never walk again. And if he did improve, the police were waiting in the wings to have him transferred into custody. Still, the thought of him lying in his bed thinking about her, made her insides feel squirmy as if she'd eaten something bad.

"Yes, I know." She forced a smile that she hoped looked more convincing than it felt. "Take care on that bike of yours."

Lance gave her a wave and headed for the exit.

Nora pushed her chair away from the desk. She could leave Archie until last or check on him now and get it over with. *He's just a kid*, she told herself and pulled her shirt down over her hips.

The curtains stood open. The glass, like a black mirror, reflected Nora's slim frame as she entered the room. A low murmur came from the television over the bed. For a moment, she thought Archie might be asleep and the chance to slip out and come back later presented itself. Nora held the door and took a shuffling backwards step when she noticed his eyes were open.

"Hey Blondie," his voice, like a phlegmy wheeze, stopped her in her tracks.

"Evening, Archie." Nora moved to the window and pulled the curtains. She could feel his gaze crawling over her backside like a slimy worm. "How're you feeling?" She kept her tone cheerful and made a show of checking her watch.

"I'm chugging along. Feeling better now my favourite nurse is here." When she let her eyes meet his, he smiled. At least that's what he seemed to be doing. One side of his mouth curved upwards while the other dragged down giving him the look of a half-frozen clown.

Nora felt a quiver of revulsion tickle her throat. *I'm over sensitive, that's what my dad always said. A little bit fey, like your Irish grandmother*, that had been another of his favourite sayings. She gave the man in the bed a tight smile. "Do you need anything?" *Please say no.*

He drew in a wet breath. "I need to take a piss." Although unable to walk, Archie still had plenty of feeling below the waist. He could move his left arm with enough dexterity to click the call button. His speech, though slushy, was clear enough to make himself understood.

"Right." Nora reached up to the shelf above the bed and grabbed a plastic bottle.

She'd known this was coming. It was as if he waited for her each night saving up his urine. Probably holding it in listening for that moment when the door whispered open just so he could force her to touch him. *He's young enough to be my son,* she reminded herself and pulled down the front of his pyjama pants.

The air in the room smelled stale with a hint of something sour. She kept her gaze averted while he filled the bottle. The liquid drill of Archie's urine drowned out the low hum of the TV. After what seemed like an eternity, the steady stream dried up.

Nora stole a glance at his face and immediately wished she hadn't. His right eye, paralysed by the trauma to his brain remained half closed while his left bulged unnaturally from its socket and roamed from her face to her breasts. The dark orb seemed to glitter with excitement.

Fighting the urge to flinch, Nora drew the bottle away. Her fingers brushed against the side of his penis which immediately squirted a spray of dark yellow urine over her wrist. "Urgh." Nora gasped, a mix of horror and revulsion.

She turned an accusing gaze on the man in the bed. Every nerve in her body jangled with the need to turn and flee. Her mouth opened and a string of curses threatened to explode. A thin line of drool ran out of the corner of Archie's lopsided smile. His seeing eye watched her with a look of excited anticipation.

Nora clamped her lips together. Suddenly denying him the satisfaction of seeing her upset seemed more important than getting the foul liquid off her hand. She turned and placed the bottle of urine on the locker next to the bed before settling Archie's pyjama bottoms, ensuring he was fully covered. As she moved, her whole being seemed focused on the spots of warm urine that covered her wrist.

When she finished settling his clothes and bedding, Nora turned slowly and walked into the little bathroom to the right of the bed. She washed her hands in the basin, leaving the door open and never glancing up at the mirror. Afraid that if she looked at herself, she'd see a middle-aged woman on the verge of tears.

After leaving the bathroom, Nora took the bottle from the locker and walked to the door. As she moved, she kept her chin up and her shoulders squared. She pushed through the door just as Archie called out, "Thanks, Blondie." A snuffling laugh followed her into the hall.

In the sluice room Nora dumped the urine and tossed the dirty bottle into the sink. She let out a long shaky breath and leaned both hands on the edge of the sink. *Don't let him make you cry,* she warned herself. *He's just a messed-up kid who's going to spend the rest of his life in a wheelchair.* But the tears flowed and with them shuddering sobs. Nothing she told herself took away the feeling of anger.

Fifteen minutes later, Nora walked out of the sluice. She glanced over at room 81 and wondered if it might be time for her to make a move. She'd given the best part of her life to general nursing, but caring for Archie left a bitter feeling in the back of her throat. Her friend Angie called geriatric nursing dull. With her eyes still puffy from tears, Nora decided dull sounded like just what she needed.

Chapter Thirty-One

Judith pulled the front door closed behind her and heard the lock click in place. Harper seemed much brighter. The panic attacks were less frequent; not as intense. She'd come a long way since those first weeks of crippling terror. Still, if Judith left without making sure the place was locked up, she'd never hear the end of it. She wished she could take the fear away, but doubted that anything would ever truly erase what happened. Harper would always bear the scars left by the Crowell brothers. They both would.

Judith let out a breath and headed for the track. One of the advantages of their new semi-rural life in Margaret River was the absence of noise. It was easier to think without the traffic and ceaseless movement of the city. But the tranquillity of the setting couldn't take away the feeling of restlessness that plagued her. A sense that she's left something unfinished. The nagging compulsion that pushed her to run.

Going for a jog, she called it. Harmless, casual – normal. What she did on the trails that cut through the three-and-a-half acres surrounding their new home was far from normal. Judith stepped onto the track and felt the familiar tingle in her chest. She dreaded and craved this moment, needed the release it brought in a way that nothing else could. She began stretching, loosening up her limbs and filling her lungs with clean air. She started off slowly enjoying the sound of her running shoes hitting the tightly packed earth. This was the moment when all the memories and the guilt could be set free and the voices of the dead filled her mind.

She increased her pace barely noticing the trees spinning past. Her sister's voice, always the first, took up residence in her head. *Please don't go. I pushed him.* Over and over the words falling into rhythm with the pounding of her feet. Then Martin, *I didn't kill your sister, you did.* Judith heard the words and forced her legs to move faster as if the guilt was something solid that could be outrun. She veered right, leaping over a fallen log, almost losing her balance. Grunting, she pushed herself forward.

Now the voices were replaced by sounds and images. Milly falling, the sickening sound when her head hit the ground. The knife entering Martin's eye, the warm spill of fluid slopping over her hand and then finally her sister's eyes, misty and lifeless, staring up at the darkening sky. Judith let out a howl and pumped her arms and legs until her heartbeat drowned out the endless reel.

She burst through the trees and skidded onto the banks of the waterway. Momentum carried her forward another metre or so, arms windmilling in an effort to stop herself toppling into the fast-moving waters of Margaret River. Arms and legs trembling, Judith bent at the waist and vomited. With each shuddering spasm, she found a small measure of calm.

It took some time for her breathing to return to normal. She dragged her arm across her mouth and grimaced. How many of these *jogs* had she taken since they'd moved to their new home? Ten? Twenty? What was the alternative? If she let the grief take hold of her, she'd break down and then what would happen to Harper? After everything she'd been through, Judith couldn't let her down. She sat on the soft grassy bank and wrapped her arms around her knees. The water whispered past, rippled by the early summer breeze. Harper was making real progress. There were times when she seemed like her old self, Judith couldn't risk shattering her girlfriend's fragile grasp on happiness. Not now.

"Judith?"

Startled, Judith whipped her head around. Harper stood in a patch of sunlight, her head tipped to one side. She opened her mouth as if to speak, but stopped. Judith turned away and ran her fingers through her hair trying to compose herself, knowing it was too late. Caught off guard, the emotions still raw and close to the surface, Harper had seen every feeling written on her face. The ragged sorrow and guilt she'd tried so long to keep inside, laid bare.

"What are you doing out here, sweetheart?" Judith tried to make her tone light, but a tremor gave her away.

"I'm looking for you. I was worried." She could hear the concern in her girlfriend's voice.

"I'm fine, I'm just having a bad day." Judith kept her eyes on the river not wanting to turn and risk another look into Harper's eyes. She heard her approach and sit beside her, her shoulder brushed Judith's arm.

"I know you're not alright, Jude." Harper's voice was soft, little more than a whisper. Judith, arms still wrapped around her legs, laid her head on her knees keeping her face turned away from her girlfriend's gaze. "I know you come out here so I won't see you upset. I know you think you're protecting me, but you don't have to."

Judith closed her eyes and swallowed. A sob was building in her chest and the effort of keeping it in made her shiver. Harper slid her arm around Judith's shoulders. She could feel the warmth coming off her skin. "I know I've been hard to live with," Harper continued. "But I'm much better now. I'm not as fragile as you think I am.

You've got to stop punishing yourself and lean on me a bit or… Or I don't know if we can make it."

Judith lifted her head. "Don't say that." She turned and looked into Harper's blue eyes, so clear and intense. "You know I love you."

"Well let me help you." Harper pulled her closer. "When I was out there." She jerked her head to the side. "Running, hiding, fighting. Deep down I knew you'd find me. If I could just survive long enough, I knew nothing would stop you. You'd find me." She reached up and brushed a strand of sweaty hair off Judith's forehead. "And you did. Now you need to lean on me."

Judith turned her body towards Harper's. She could feel all the pain and anguish bubbling up to the surface. This time, she didn't try to hold back. She pressed her face into Harper's shoulder. She smelled like fresh linen and honey, a scent that reminded Judith of childhood and breakfast in bed. She breathed in the comforting aroma and let the tears come. She cried for her mother and for Milly, for the terrible aching loss. There were even tears for herself, some of grief, but also relief.

When the weeping finally ended, Harper pulled away and stood. "Come on. Let's go home." She offered Judith her hand. "We've spent enough time out in the great outdoors."

If you enjoyed this book, please let others know by leaving a quick review on Amazon. Also, if you spot anything untoward in the paperback, get in touch. We strive for the best quality and appreciate reader feedback.

editor@thebookfolks.com

www.thebookfolks.com

Also by Anna Willett:

**BACKWOODS RIPPER
UNWELCOME GUESTS
FORGOTTEN CRIMES
CRUELTY'S DAUGHTER
SMALL TOWN NIGHTMARE
VENGEANCE BLIND**

Printed in Great Britain
by Amazon